ISOLATION

SARAH K. STEPHENS

BLOODHOUND
— BOOKS —

ALSO BY SARAH K. STEPHENS

It Was Always You

∽

The Anniversary

For Mom, always my first reader

One thousand steps.

That's how many it takes to cross from one end of our home to the other. I know it's strange that it's such an exact number. But there are lots of strange things happening right now, and the fact that I can walk from our dinner parlor to the end of the kitchen in a perfectly round number seems to be a little less weird than everything else.

But, if that bothers you, I can give you other measurements.

375 seconds. Six minutes and fifteen seconds.

59 breaths.

10 rooms to cross.

25 windows to look out of.

5 people to avoid.

Except today is different. Today, I only get to 785 steps before I see the body.

"Four people to avoid." This new fact slithers out of my mouth before I can replace it with something more appropriate, like "Oh no!" or "Help!" or "Are you okay?" even though I can clearly see that they aren't.

Their pale white fingers clench into a claw that grips at

nothing. And there's blood. So, so much blood that I can barely see two eyes blankly staring through the wet curtain of it.

I shouldn't be able to count, but I do and it only takes me 523 steps to run upstairs, past my bedroom and into the panic room. I curl myself into a ball against the soft soundproof walls, pulling my hands over my eyes like a toddler who thinks nobody can see them if they can't see anything themselves.

And that's where I wait for what I know is coming next.

Coming for all of us.

1

DAY 1
BRENNA

I take a sip of coffee and snap open the paper. Mark used to tease me about being old-fashioned when I insisted that we keep getting the paper delivered.

"Everything is online now," he'd said. "And besides, we live so far out it doesn't seem fair to make someone come and deliver it."

But I'd held firm, and so for the last ten years we've had the paper dropped off each morning in our box at the end of our drive. Until he wasn't able to, Mark would go and get it for me each day before breakfast.

The headlines are the same as the days before, with slight changes in the number of cases reported and the political firestorm of blame swirling around. I automatically skim them, push them to the back of my mind and suppress the surge of bile they inevitably trigger, and turn instead to the business section. One of our main competitors, Digital Global, was supposed to put out a big patch to their software today and I'm wondering if *The Times* got a scoop on how insufficient it is. Or rather, I'm wondering if they decided to print the information my company leaked purposefully to diminish the significance of this supposed improvement.

The business section is smaller today, and looking over the content reveals nothing related to my company, Chronos, or to Digital Global. Most are estimates of the financial impact of recent events, and I don't need to read the paper for that info. The notifications on my phone for our stock investments keep pinging away, each share price lower than the next.

I decide to put the paper away and try to refocus on something positive. My therapist keeps pushing mindfulness training, but for the $200 an hour I'm paying her I should really be getting more than "sit still and listen to your breathing" as the solution to all my problems.

There are pictures of Felix and Daphne taped to our subzero fridge, along with a smattering of drawings they've done over the last few years. I will my mind to focus on them, but all I can manage to do is push down the surge of dread that's threatening to overtake me like a smothering pillow.

Margot will be getting the children up soon.

And then they'll be here, in our huge sunny kitchen with the Italian black marble and the breakfast nook, scarfing down cereal and singing songs and poking each other in the shoulders until cereal is everywhere.

How much cereal do we have? I think. *Do we need to get more?*

I try to take another sip of coffee, but my hand trembles as I bring the cup to my mouth. If I'm not careful, I'm going to scare them. I need to get a handle on myself.

"Brenna?" The voice trickles in like the sunlight through the gauzy curtains our decorator picked out last spring, when I needed a distraction from the other remodel we were doing.

I look up and see Margot, eyes puffy from sleep and her dark hair coming loose from the sloppy top knot she pulls her hair back in at bedtime. She looks like she slept deeply, and as I watch her come into the kitchen from the hallway she reaches up and rubs her eye with her fist, like a baby might do.

She's so much younger than you, I remind myself. Be kind to her.

"I was finishing my coffee," I tell her as I pour the rest of my cup into the sink and set my empty mug on the counter.

She and I both stare at it for a moment, realizing perhaps at the same time that it is going to stay there until one of us washes it. Greta, our long-time housekeeper, left yesterday to go back to Scranton, Pennsylvania, to take care of her aging mother. She said she didn't want to risk being away from her if everything went into lockdown.

Margot steps towards me, but I reach out to take the sponge before she can get to it. I squeeze out some dish soap and scrub the mug. It has a picture of Donald Duck on the front, and I cover his orange bill and ridiculous sailor suit in sudsy water so I can't see it for a moment. Mark was always a big fan of Looney Tunes, and I can almost taste the scent of his aftershave mixed with the bitter aroma of his dark roast coffee as he'd drink it in the morning, tan and strong in his shirt sleeves and sneaking quick kisses from me as I rushed to get ready.

"Here, let me do it," Margot says, and she reaches her arms around my waist and grabs the cup from me. I feel her hip bones press into the soft flesh of my backside, and her breath comes softly at the nape of my neck.

But then there's the patter of little feet on the floor, and Daphne bursts into the room, followed by the more solid steps of Felix.

"I woke up by myself," Daphne announces, her arms outstretched in a joyous Y.

Margot moves fluidly away from me and over to the fridge, where she pretends to scan the shelves for milk.

And like that, we're strangers again.

2

MARGOT

"Just pick one, please," I tell Daphne.

I'm holding up two dresses, one covered in a bright red strawberry print and sleeveless, the other a rich cream velvet with a hunter green sash to tie at the back. Both are totally inappropriate for a seven-year-old girl to wear on a weekday in the middle of March, but I don't care. These are the first two I grabbed out of the closet when Brenna asked me to help with Daphne while she tended to something Felix needed.

I'm a nurse, not a nanny.

Although, of course, I want to be helpful. Don't get me wrong. I'm reading the headlines too, and I know these are extraordinary times, unprecedented days, or whatever other phrase you want to use to describe what's happening right now in the world. That's partly why I've gotten in the habit of waking the kids up in the morning, while Brenna has a chance to actually eat something for breakfast—although more likely she'll just chug a huge mug of coffee—before she heads into the office.

We're all going to need to be a bit more flexible in the days to come.

Maybe a *lot* more flexible.

Daphne stares intently at my offering, her cherub-like face framed in soft golden-blond curls. She blinks at me and tilts her head to the side in deep concentration. She is an absolutely gorgeous child, and I'm convinced this is why she's developed certain—habits, you might say—that make the adults in her life a little too gullible.

Correction. *Most* of the adults.

I grew up with four sisters. I know when I'm being played.

"Okay, it's the strawberry one." I swing the velvet dress back into the closet and shift the straps of Daphne's dress off the hanger, knowing full well what's about to happen.

"No, not the strawberries. I want the other one," Daphne chirps up, all decisiveness suddenly.

"I don't know," I tell her. "You seemed like you weren't sure just a moment ago. I don't want you taking forever to get ready. I have other stuff I need to do."

"I promise. I'll get ready *so* fast. Pretty please, let me wear it!"

I move the other dress from the closet and hand it off to the seven-year-old. Daphne promptly moves to the private en suite bathroom that's attached to her bedroom and closes the door.

I don't wait. I could cook my mother eggs and pancakes—by myself—by the time I was seven. There's no reason Daphne can't dress herself. And before I'm even halfway down the hallway I hear the click of the shoes she's managed to put on along with her chosen dress, with a tied bow at the back and everything.

"I'm ready," she announces to no one in particular.

Just then, Brenna appears around the corner with Felix in tow. He has dark rings under his eyes, like he didn't sleep well for the last several weeks. Brenna hasn't mentioned anything specifically to me, but I've been able to gather that there's something wrong at school.

When I first moved in nine months ago, I thought the eaves

under the window of my room were moaning in the wind—sure, the house is renovated beyond an inch of its life, but it's still old in its bones—until I realized it wasn't the house. It was Felix.

"You look gorgeous," Brenna says to Daphne.

And it's true. She does.

"I did it all by myself," Daphne informs her mother. Brenna glances at me.

"Did you now?" she tells her daughter. "Aren't you such a big girl!"

Daphne beams and then click-clacks off to somewhere else in the house.

Brenna, Felix, and I are left in an awkward trio in the hallway.

"I could dress myself by the time I was in kindergarten," Felix informs us solemnly.

My point, exactly.

...

Mark Stone was the unofficial poster boy for renewable energy tech that "*looks* as good as it *does* good." At least, that's what I read online when I was first hired for this job. I already knew who Mark Stone was—he was a media darling before he got sick, and everyone in the US knew the name to the same extent—but after coming over to Brenna's office in town for my interview I did a deep internet dive. There were so many profiles of him looking gorgeous and fit, staring out into the distance in his $3,000 suits as he contemplated the industry his electrical engineering degree and his sheer chutzpah had helped create, that I wasn't prepared for what I found when Brenna eventually hired me and I came to the house.

And let me be clear. I'm an excellent nurse. I've worked in nursing homes and hospice care and the NICU. I might be under thirty but I've got the experience. I know what bodies and minds look like when they're wasting away.

But even still, seeing Mark Stone that first time in contrast to the Mark Stone I saw in those photo spreads and articles? It was almost painful.

Getting into the house was a complicated process to begin with. I had to buzz in at the front gate, and then drive my beat-up Chevy Corsica down their winding front path until I came to the crescent-shaped curve with several parking spaces for visitors. If you've ever seen any of the Pride and Prejudice movie adaptations, where Elizabeth Bennett rides up with her aunt and uncle to the gates of Pemberley, then you know what it felt like coming around a bend on that wooded road and then suddenly seeing this palatial mansion sitting right on a lake and surrounded by pastures and fields where chestnut brown horses were grazing. It was like biting into an overripe fruit that spilled out luxury all across your mouth and down onto your shirt.

And you might have choked on it a little.

Brenna met me at the door, a real vision of cool executive style in a creamy blouse, sleek navy slacks, and a fresh blow-out that made her blond hair shine in the sunshine that poured in onto the stone doorstep.

"Did you find us okay?" were her first words to me at the entrance, and I had to laugh because there was a huge sign at the initial turn off from the main road, and then subsequent signs after that, announcing that Granfield Estate was to the right or left (and deliveries go to the back). It was impossible to mistake that I was anywhere else. Or that most of the people coming to visit this ridiculously opulent house were a different class than the people who lived there.

Brenna gave me a tight look that I smiled into.

"I'm sorry to laugh. It's just that your house is pretty unmistakable," I explained.

I was tempted to say more, but I know from working with so many families under pressure that senseless chatter is a burden they have to endure, not a welcome distraction. Every day they have friends and neighbors and family buzzing around them, too uncomfortable to let a pause slip in and for the reality of the situation to shift forward in their conversation. I'm not like that. I don't mind silence.

I watched Brenna's face as she took my coat and hung it behind a nearly invisible closet door in the front hallway. Sure enough, as I let the quiet sink in around us for a few seconds I saw her eyes soften and a small smile play at the corners of her mouth.

"It was a museum for a while, you know," she noted, and started moving down the hallway, motioning for me to follow with a long elegant arm. "They were going to tear it down, if you can believe that, and build a shopping mall. But we were able to buy it just in time. We've tried to preserve a lot of the original structure of the house, but with modern amenities added in. It's been a passion project for Mark and me."

We'd been walking along the west wing of the house as Brenna talked, and at the mention of her husband we found ourselves outside a heavy oak door that would have been a perfect fit for some period drama with corsets and gas lighting except for the glowing keypad in place of a door handle.

Brenna explained, "We renovated the rooms to make them as normal-seeming as possible, but with the assurance that Mark would be protected too. After everything that's happened..." She paused, and I took a deep breath. I waited.

We were still standing outside the door. She gave her head a small shake, like she was dislodging her original thought.

"Here we are," she said, slipping a plastic card out of her pants pocket and holding it against the keypad, like you would in a fancy hotel. There was a soft whir and a click, and the door came ajar.

Brenna pushed the door open, and I found myself in a softly lit room filled with overstuffed chairs and a plush baby blue couch. The room looked entirely normal, except that there were metal bars installed along the walls at hip height, running around the length of the room. Two bright red buttons glowed dimly from the opposing corners.

"This was Mark's sitting room for a while. We'd come in here, after dinner, and relax together. Things moved so quickly though. We didn't get to use it much." Brenna reached out a hand as she was talking and touched one of the metal bars. It must have shocked her, perhaps from the static in the air, because she pulled herself back as though she'd just been bit.

We went through to the next room in the West side of the house, which was still decorated like an interior designer's vision board with a wallpaper in deep teal that had a sort of sheen to it and expensive long-hanging curtains over the windows, but the room itself was almost entirely bare except for a piece in the far corner that looked like some sort of hybrid desk and bed.

Brenna kept walking, and pulled out her key card once again to hold against a pad in the furthest door. The door opened like the first, with a soft whoosh, but this time I knew he was inside.

The smell was unmistakable. It was the odor of skin shrouded in sheets for too long, of a body holding one position for too many unrestful hours. Of a mind chipping away one piece at a time until all that's left is a tiny kernel of the original's brilliance.

It was the smell of debilitation and disease and despair, all rolled into one.

I stepped inside willingly. This was what I was here to do.

3

TOBIAS

Horses can smell fear.

When I walk into the stables this morning, Julie and Jasmine snuffle in their stalls like they have bad colds. I hear a hoof stomp on the ground, followed by another in the adjoining stall. The unrest spreads to the other horses, who all start to rustle. There's the distinctive scrape of their sleeping blankets against the smooth wood of their stall doors.

Nobody is happy.

I think about stepping back outside, into the clean air of the pasture and the acre or two that separates the stables from the main house, but my girls need to be fed and brushed down. They're waiting for me, and like a parent who has to put on a brave face for their children when there's danger looming around their little family unit, I shake my shoulders and unclench my jaw and try to act normal.

The underarms of my shirt are already drenched, even though it's only seven in the morning and cool outside for the season. I tell my body to behave.

That'll teach me to wake up and check the headlines.

I go to Jasmine first, because she's the natural matriarch.

Julie might be technically older, but Jasmine is the leader of their little pack. She eyes me as I come up at the entrance to her stall, and I whisper the same words I say to her each morning, like I always do.

"There's a good girl," I tell her. "There's a gorgeous Jasmine. You're the queen of horses, you are."

I put my hand flat against her neck and feel the pulse of her body vibrate through my skin. She pauses for a second, and her nostrils flare as she sniffs the air, but she must decide that I'm calmed down and that the world is back in order, because she turns and nuzzles her cheek into my shoulder.

I push the hair from her eyes, scratch gently behind her ears, and then move to pick up the brushes in the corner of her stall and take off her sleeping blanket.

The sounds from the other horses continue to ratchet up, but as I lead Jasmine out into the main area of the stable for her morning rub down she must have communicated something in the pitch of her shoulders or the twist of her body, because they all quiet down and wait patiently as I loop Jasmine's bridle into the fixed post and then go around to put their morning oats and hay in their troughs.

Jasmine's the only horse I feed by hand, which I do before I start to brush her sleek chestnut body.

The routine helps me too, and as I get into the rhythm of the strokes along her broad back and down her flank, I feel something release in my brain and a sense of security washes over me.

The world couldn't collapse. Not when there were still creatures as magnificent as this willing to let us care for them, even though one kick from their leg or the quick toss of a head could kill me.

Not when there was this type of trust in the world.

I look out the stable doors as I'm finishing, and the mist from the tall grass in the fields is already burning off as the sun rises in the distance.

I feel calmer, and the sweat that soaked through my shirt is starting to dry. For a moment I wonder if I should go up to my apartment above the old mill barn around the back and change into a fresh one, but I glance at my watch—it's eight—and decide to stay put. The extra stable hands will be arriving soon, and they'll need their instructions for the day.

It was Mark Stone who hired me way back when they first bought the museum. He had been invested in me from the beginning, even though I wasn't the perfect fit and my résumé had a few blips on it that I could explain but didn't want to. Especially not to a man like him.

They only had two horses back then—Julie and Jasmine, my girls—and the others were added on over the years to make a family for Julie and Jasmine to tend to. At least, that's what Mark told me once when he stopped by for one of his daily rides.

"Horses are like people, aren't they, Tobias?" He'd given me a knowing wink, because of course I knew more about horses than he did. I'd grown up around them my entire life, whereas he'd only started riding after he earned his first and second million, and decided that golf wasn't his thing, but that being an equestrian might be the rich-person activity he could tolerate. He'd told me that as well, sitting together one afternoon as the sun set over his land and sipping chilled beers from my fridge. He was never proud or condescending. Mark may have owned every piece, but he also knew he was a visitor in the stables. "They need a family."

Thinking about Mark takes my mind wandering to other places, and I feel that pulse of sweat flash over me again. *I should call my mother*, I think.

What's ten years of radio silence during a time like this?

14

She's probably still listed in the phone book. Or online somewhere.

I could find her, if I tried hard enough.

Something moves in the distance, underneath the long limbs of the grass. It's making a straight line through the field, towards us. Me and my horses.

It's probably a fox. They've been coming closer and closer to the stables at night, and a few times I've found little nicks at the back of a horse's legs, from where a fox came in and decided to play boss for the evening. It's why we've started locking up the stables at night, and closing everything up nice and secure like. Luckily it's been cool enough that the horses are okay with it, and don't need the stream of a breeze flowing through as they sleep.

I'm not sure what we'll do once summer really comes.

The creature is getting closer. I can tell by the bend of the long grass out in the distance. I glance over at the shovel leaned against the front wall, next to the extra buckets and lead lines. I could grab it in a split second if I needed to.

My phone buzzes in my back pocket. I keep my gaze on the field, but then tip the front of my baseball cap down to shield my eyes from the glare of the sun's rays streaming through the stable door, and pull out the tiny glowing screen.

The alert on my phone is unfamiliar. I have notifications for some of the apps I use—social media accounts where I chat mainly with other horse people and a few political sites. But this is different. The icon in the text box is red, and the words are crisp and blunt, like the edge of my shovel.

"Lockdown in Full Effect" it says.

I glance up, but the creature in the field is gone.

4

BRENNA

I decide to put on lipstick before I see Mark. It's a NARS that's been knocking around in the back of my makeup drawer in the bathroom we used to share. The name of the color is something mildly salacious, like "Pillow Pink" or "Vulva Red," but I can't quite remember and the label on the bottom of the tube has rubbed off.

It's going to be a hard day at work. The shareholders will be barking down the lines at my assistant. I already have ten new messages pinging at my phone, notifying me that I have my work cut out for me today to try to keep this floating world of my company from sinking.

I throw the rest of my toiletries back into one of the drawers, where they rattle around with some of Mark's forgotten items. An old-fashioned razor with its slick blade bent into the handle. An old bottle of cologne Felix bought for him at the school's Little Elf shop last holiday season. A wristband of meditation beads that he wore more for fashion than meditation.

My husband was many things. *Is* many things.

But a calm mind isn't one of them.

I'd already been in once to see Mark, when I first woke up. I like to start my day by seeing how he's doing. But that early in the morning he's usually groggy from the sleep medication his physician prescribed starting a few months ago to help him sleep through the pain, and I've found that making a second visit before I head to the office gives us a chance to connect again before I leave for the day. Before I turn his care over to Margot.

My hand shakes a little as I think of her name. I feel myself blush, like some middle schooler with a crush. There's a smear off the upper corner of my mouth and so I wipe my mistake away with a tissue. Staring at myself in the mirror, I think that I look like a composite of other women, patched together. The last few years have left their mark, and the past nine months have pressed themselves under my eyes, against the hollow skin of my jaw. Sometimes it feels like my body is hanging off my bones, waiting to drop to the floor and finally rest in a heap of everything I won't let myself feel.

My phone pings in the back pocket of my wool pants. They have a silk lining, so the fabric doesn't itch. They cost more than my monthly rent, back when I first founded Chronos.

A sick feeling rises in my stomach and so I start moving, away from the mirror and through our—*my*—bedroom and towards the west wing where my husband is waiting for me.

I ignore my phone. The moment I start responding to that piece of my life is the moment I'm lost for the day.

Nobody can know how grateful I am to get to leave every day and pretend that my life is something different for eight hours—sometimes ten, on a rough patch of release days—before I return home and have to put on the shell that lets me function as a wife and a mother without cracking from the pressure of caring for other people.

I hear footsteps on the stairs as I turn right towards Mark's set of rooms. Even though the sun is out, the light streaming through the glass dome in the center of the front hall above the main staircase is muted the way light filters through a swimming pool.

Felix is at the bottom, his backpack strapped across his shoulders like he's preparing for war. I give him a little smile, which he may not even be able to see given the dim light and how far away from him I am.

"I'm going to check on Daddy, and then we'll get you and your sister to school," I tell him, my voice flipped into a bright song.

My phone pings again, sending a jolt through my body.

"Can I come with you?"

The muscles in my stomach clench.

"Sure, sweetheart." I move down a few steps and extend my hand to my son. Despite all of Greta's best efforts to making fortifying dishes of grits and potatoes au gratin and macaroni and cheese, Felix is still whippet-thin and sallow with dark blunt bangs—which he cut himself one night alone in his bathroom—and hunched shoulders. Margot told me once that he looked like he was nine going on ninety.

I had to correct her. Felix is eleven, not nine.

And then I felt like a terrible mother for implicitly agreeing with everything else she'd said.

Felix's face brightens and he skips up the stairs, leaving his backpack on the ground by the front door. He holds on to my hand as we walk the short distance to the first keypad, passing Margot along the way as she returns from her morning rounds with Mark. We give each other a quick nod when we pass, but Felix ignores Margot and keeps his own eyes fixed ahead.

I squeeze his hand. "She's taking good care of Dad, don't you think?"

My son doesn't respond, and a few seconds later I have to let go of him in order to retrieve the key card from my left side pocket.

Felix shudders into life. "Can I do the keypad?"

"Not today," I say as I press the card to the door and the locks sweep themselves open.

I reach out and take my son's hand again as we cross the two other rooms before we come up to where his father is lying, machines and tubes leeching out from all sides.

But as we enter the room, something is wrong.

The whir of the monitors and pumps are missing, making the space where my husband should be resting entirely silent. Mark's bed is empty.

"Oh my God," I cry out before I can catch myself. Felix's hand tightens in my grip, and almost instantly I feel his palm slick with sweat.

"Where's Dad?" he asks.

"Maybe Margot put him in his chair?" My mind scrambles for some explanation. "Maybe Margot's with him?"

"We just passed her," Felix replies matter-of-factly.

I scan the room, but everything is a blank space. The hospital-style bed and monitors, the intravenous stand. Empty. There's no sign of Mark anywhere, except for the rumpled sheets on the bed and the side railing on the right side, which has been brought down.

So he must have gotten out of bed, somehow, rather than having someone carry him?

All of this seems ridiculous.

My phone pings again, and I finally pull it out and look at it, ignoring the judgmental glance from Felix that says, "How can you worry about that stupid thing when my father is *missing*!"

There are so many notifications that my screen has loaded them, one on top of another, like an accordion pleat. But the very first one hasn't been replaced, even though it came in twenty minutes ago.

It's not from my assistant or my CFO or anyone at my company.

It's a state-wide alert that we are all in lockdown. No one is to leave their homes. No one is meant to be on the roads. The National Guard is being deployed.

We are at the epicenter of an international pandemic, apparently.

I glance from my screen to my son's face, who looks at me with such a vivid gaze of disappointment that I have to catch my breath.

"We're locked in, aren't we?" he says, all statement and no question.

"I...We..." I fumble to put my phone back into my pocket, but it won't slip inside despite the expensive fabric and the hand-sewn lining.

I run around the room, feeling terror shudder through my body and making my movements jerky. My limbs keep bumping into edges and surfaces that I misjudge as I navigate the space. I look inside the adjoining and handicap-equipped bathroom, but it is empty and smells sterile. Like no one has used it for a long time.

I can't do this without Mark.

I can't be here, with them, together with the end in sight without my husband.

Where is he?

I come back out into the room, and an intense pressure grips at my chest and temples to the point that I think I'm going to hyperventilate.

In the corner of the room, by the door we entered, is a figure backlit by the light of the curtains. It's clear from their posture that they're holding a body across their arms.

Felix walks towards them, extending his hand as though he's about to touch a holy relic. The figure in the doorway moves in the direction of my son, and the size of this person looming over the room swallows Felix in shadow. A stab of recognition slices through the base of my skull: someone got in again.

Someone broke into my husband's safe place. This time they did it right.

They are here to blackmail us, or kidnap us. Or take revenge for something Mark did before he became so sick.

Or after, I correct myself.

Not again, I want to scream. Not again.

"Get the fuck away from my family!" I hurl my body into the room, cutting off Felix as he approaches this monster holding my husband's inert body like a rag doll.

"Get out!" I scream. I clench my hands into two tight fists and prepare to do whatever I can so that Felix can leave the room safely and run to get help from Margot. To take Daphne into the panic room we didn't have a chance to use last time.

The figure lurches back into a stream of sunshine and the smudges that were their face come into clear focus. I know this person. I know who has my husband.

I shake my head, trying to clear my vision and letting the adrenaline seep out of my body and into the air around me.

"I came after the lockdown orders," Tobias says, a judgy tinge at the tip of his words, like he's critiquing me for not being with Mark. "I didn't want him to be alone."

I look at Tobias, then Felix. Both of them stare back at me intently.

Finally, I look at my husband, and see that Mark's eyes are bright and clear. "Brenna, everything's okay," he tells me. Some of his words are slurred a little, but like I learned the special sounds that Felix and Daphne made when they were first learning to speak, I can understand what my husband says as he loses his ability to talk.

"I was so worried," I tell him.

"He wanted to go out into the sunshine," Tobias gives as way of explanation.

He puts Mark gently back on his bed, and I hit the buzzer by Mark's pillows that automatically calls Margot to the room. I start putting the different tubes and monitor pads back in place.

Tobias stands on the edge of the room. There are two dark impressions where his shoes left mud stains on the carpet.

"Get out," I hiss.

"I'm sorry..." Tobias begins.

"Sweetheart," Mark starts to say.

"I said, get out," I repeat.

I let my eyes fall on Tobias, and then onto Felix. I try to soften them as I look at my son, but it's hard to do.

There's a high-pitched click followed by rustling behind Tobias, and Margot appears through the doorframe and pushes herself into the room.

She turns to Tobias for a moment and then comes over to Mark's bed, snapping over her shoulder, "What did you do?"

Felix just stands in the center of the room, not moving. He stares at his father, at the wrist of his right arm.

Tobias has already left, leaving his trail of dirty footprints behind him.

And that's when I see it. I turn Mark's wrist over, gingerly, and move it out of the pool of red soaking into the sheets around it. The wound doesn't look entirely fresh, but it's still oozing blood. A straight line lies along his wrist, in parallel to the bones of his forearm.

"Who did this?" I ask Mark. "Who hurt you?"

Mark doesn't respond. He just closes his eyes.

I look at Margot, and then my son.
Neither of them look back.

5

FELIX

Daphne thinks this is all just one big extended summer break.

When Mom told her she didn't have to go to school today—that we weren't going to school for at least a few weeks, in fact—she actually did a little spin-hop thing and then put her arms in the air like she was a cheerleader in a movie.

"Woohoo!" she cried out.

I can't believe she's the only other kid I will see for the indeterminate future. I'm already dying a little inside.

After the news, I retreated to the third floor, which is kind of my space. "My lair." That's what Mom refers to it as sometimes, right before she reaches out and tousles my hair like Dad used to be able to. It doesn't feel the same when she does it.

I don't necessarily like the term "lair"—I'm not some evil genius in a comic book movie—but I have migrated a lot of my things up to the old apartment Daphne's baby nanny used to occupy. I have my books, and my laptop and a few video game systems set up with a big TV screen, although I'm not much of a video gamer. I think Mom and Dad bought them for me a few years ago, hoping that I'd go online and make friends with other kids like me.

And my telescope. I have that set up at the far window, facing out into the fields and stables towards the east. I know it's the east because, when I sleep up here sometimes, that's where the sun comes in first.

I climb up from where I've been sitting, flipping through an old Biology textbook one of our nannies must have left behind from an online college class they were taking, and move over to the window. The eyepiece fits perfectly into the smooth edges of my sphenoid bone, like it was meant to be there.

Looking out, I don't see anyone. Only green fields stretching out for what seems like forever, until they're met by the deep green edge of the forest. I see the stables, and the open barn doors, and the fenced-in pen where Tobias or one of his handlers will work with the horses or saddle Mom up for a ride.

Since Dad got sick, it seems like Mom's taken over everything that Dad used to do.

Almost everything.

I keep scanning the horizon, hoping to spot a hawk or a blue heron, maybe. One time I saw a hawk swoop down from the sky and snatch a field mouse straight out of the tall grass.

It was over in a few seconds, like a snap of God's fingers that said, "Little mouse, it's your time."

It's a real grown-up telescope. Dad told me so when he and Mom gave it to me for my ninth birthday.

"This isn't some kid-friendly version, Felix," he'd said. "So make sure to treat it with respect. It's a scientific instrument. Not a plaything."

That's my dad.

Correction. That *was* my dad.

I could tell Mom was really shaken up about everything that happened in Dad's room. I know Tobias and Dad were pretty good friends, and they'd hang out sometimes at the stables in the evening. Even after Dad had to stay in bed most of the time, Tobias would stop by to chat and give Dad updates on the horses.

I'd hear them talking about Jasmine or Julie. Sometimes whether one of the new studs was ready to send out for breeding or something else equally scientific and gross at the same time.

I saw Dad's cut on his wrist before Mom did. I should have told her that he was bleeding, but I didn't. I think I wanted to see what she'd do if she found out herself.

In the past, when I've told her about awful things happening, I could see on her face that she didn't quite believe me. That she thought I had something to do with it.

Dad never looked at me that way.

I press the eyepiece further into my skin, hoping it'll leave an impression on my cheek and forehead that will look like a monocle. I read in one of my books that Louis Pasteur used to go around his lab with permanent dents in his face from looking through a microscope for so many hours.

But pressing into the telescope doesn't seem to help me see anything. In lockdown, there's going to be even less to look at.

Mom. Dad. Daphne. Margot. Tobias. Greta.

I'm counting the human beings I'll be seeing for these next weeks.

No, Greta left already.

Who else? The horses, I guess.

Is that really it? Just five people to watch now.

I look out at the fields again. There's a dark smudge moving across the pathway from the house to the stables. I blink, not sure of what I'm seeing.

I shift the telescope's focus away from the field, and pull the viewer closer and refocus on the smudge and the small cloud of dust kicking up at the back as it travels across the viewer.

When I shift the focus, it takes me a moment but I recognize who it is. Darren, the guy who handles our gardens and the other landscaping stuff for the most part, is driving down the connecting road between the stables and the tool barn in the little golf-cart vehicle he uses to navigate around the property. One time I asked Mom why we needed so many people working at the house all the time, and she said that big houses need big help. Or something like that. There are always things that need doing and fixing, she'd said.

My mom's hands are really smooth, like ivory soap carved into the shape of a woman's hand. She doesn't cook, or clean, or touch much of anything, really. Just buttons on her phone or laptop or the keypad to Dad's rooms.

I'd forgotten about Darren.

I move from the telescope, pull open the window, and yell to him over the cool stream of air that rushes in. "You're not supposed to be here!"

He doesn't look up from his seat in the cart.

Darren stands up when he gets to the stable and leaves the cart parked in front. He glances around him, like he's trying to see who's spotted him in the unfamiliar territory of the horses. Usually he stays clear of Tobias' area. They don't really like each other.

I keep looking as Darren turns, wipes a hand across his forehead, and I see him weave as he finds his footing on the gravel drive, and then walk in through the open door of the stables. But not before I try again.

"Get out!" I tell him.

But he doesn't turn around. Instead, I watch Darren move further into the shadows of the stables until he blends in with the dark edges.

Six people.

There are six people for me to watch.

6

MARGOT

I slink into bed like a feral cat, whiplike and then all tense, vigilant energy. Today was spent trying to keep my patient comfortable and safe, despite the nervous energy swirling around him.

Anxiety is the worst thing for someone who is slowly, painfully dying. I keep trying to tell Brenna that, but she doesn't seem to listen. Or maybe she can't listen. Her worry seeps off her like an expensive perfume, and I know Mark can sense it anytime she's around.

And now, with us being told to shelter at home while this wild virus rips through our country, I think the tension in the air is going to hit a point where Mark won't be able to breathe with the weight of it all.

Today wasn't the first time he'd tried to harm himself. Whenever I take his pulse I feel with my fingertips the soft ridges of scars. He's been creative in the past, finding edges on his bedside railings where the metal wasn't welded perfectly, or the ragged lines of IV tubing that we used to store in his bedside table drawer. Apparently, if you pull unfinished plastic against skin you can tear it like a knife would. You just have to be persistent.

And Mark Stone is nothing if not persistent.

My room sits on the second floor of the main house of Granfield estate. It faces the west wing, and from my window I see the hard angles of the building as it bends into the side structure of the house where Mark lives. Brenna's bedroom is on my side of the house too, although she seems to sleep in the sitting room outside Mark's bedroom at least a few times a week.

I know because I've gone to find her, in the middle of the night when the loneliness just won't go away, and she's not in her bedroom. Those nights, I find myself inexplicably wandering into the children's section of the house and peering in as their small bodies breathe that satisfying sleep that children only seem to experience. Sometimes though, Daphne's door is closed already or Felix's room is locked and I have to stare at the dim edges of their nightlights seeping out underneath the bottom crack of their doors. Even then, it's some comfort. Sometimes Felix has his fits, and I've learned that it's best to leave him to it. Nursing him through it only seems to make it worse.

The bedding I sink into isn't my own. It came with the job. Egyptian cotton and some-hundred-count sheets in a crisp stylish grey with a bright white comforter. The rest of my room is the same style. A slim modern desk. A dresser in shabby chic white that matches the blue swirls in the wallpaper. When I first came here, I thought maybe Brenna had made this room just for me, thinking of the ocean and heavy wild skies, but when I asked her she said that Mark was really the designer of the two of them. He'd chosen most of the pieces and color schemes for this section of the house. Brenna only oversaw the most recent renovation, the one she did when Mark was too sick to do it himself.

I close my eyes, exhausted but satisfied at the same time. I was a good nurse today. I wrapped Mark's wound, changed his bandage when needed, measured his vitals, chatted with him a little. I've gotten pretty good at understanding what he's trying to say. I hope I made him as comfortable as possible. I hope I didn't let the news affect my work.

We're trapped here, but Mark doesn't need to know that.

I must be drifting off when I hear a creak outside my door. The house has lots of sounds, and I've come to know them pretty well, but I don't recognize this one. It's like someone snapped a board of wood, and then tried to muffle the sound with their body. I throw off my covers and rush to the door, ready to confront whoever might be there.

I didn't lock my bedroom at first when I arrived at Granfield House, but after Tobias crept in a few times—sleepwalking, he said—I started locking myself in tight. He never touched me, and I'd start awake to find him standing in the center of my room, staring off into the distance or looking intently at a corner. It was more than creepy.

When I fling the door open though, no one is there. Only the soft settling of the house around me. Thick carpets and brass fittings. The chandelier in the main stairway catches in the moonlight that's streaming through the windows.

But then I hear it. That same, insistent crack shattering the quiet.

I follow the sound down the hallway, away from the main entrance and towards the children's area of the house. My feet are bare, and the soft nap of the carpet absorbs the sounds of my footsteps so I can move silently through the house, like a ghost of myself.

Felix and Daphne's rooms are in the same hallway, caddy-corner to each other. I pass by a few nondescript rooms, including Mark's old office and a library-like room with tall bookcases in light, Scandinavian wood and a refurbished fireplace that's been converted to gas instead of wood-burning. I don't think it gets used all that often. I've never seen anyone in there, except for Greta when she would dust and vacuum it.

The snapping wood comes once more, and I'm certain now that it's coming somewhere from the children's rooms, although I can't tell whether it's Felix, or Daphne's, or something else close by. Both doors to the children's rooms are cracked, with the light from their nightlights glowing gently through the smaller openings. I'm almost to Felix's door when I feel someone grab me by the shoulder, and twist my body around.

I let out a scream, and the hand moves to cover my mouth and stifle me.

I try to focus my gaze on the form in front of me, and finally I get my eyes to settle on their face. The terror inside my gut immediately dissipates.

It's only Brenna.

I take in her expression, and that pit inside me ratchets itself up my throat again. She's pale, and in the moonlight her chiseled features give her a gaunt appearance. I blink, because for a moment all I can see is the skull beneath her skin.

"I need your help," she whispers. "I need you now."

"What's wrong?" I automatically blush as a hint of satisfaction creeps into my question, because hearing her say she needs me is everything.

"It's Mark."

She turns and starts to half walk, half run down the hallway and down the staircase, towards the west wing.

"He was fine when I did my pre-bedtime check," I assure her. He couldn't have hurt himself again, I think. Usually it's several weeks between episodes. And I'd surveyed that entire room, looking for anything that might be used to self-injure.

Although, I remind myself, Mark's proved really creative in the past.

"Did he hurt himself again?" I follow-up, trying to move my tired body forward to keep up with her.

Brenna doesn't respond. She just keeps walking, until we're at the keypad and she's pushing the heavy door open and we're inside Mark's sanctum of care.

But I hear what's happening before I even step through the doorway.

"Someone was here!" Mark's voice carries through the adjoining rooms. "Someone tried to kill me!"

It's the loudest I've heard him speak. Ever.

His voice is raspy from underuse, and some of his words merge into each other. But, even still, what he's saying is unmistakable.

When we come into the room, he's writhing on the ground. We installed hand and foot straps a while ago, but we only use them when we absolutely need to—when Mark's too agitated or angry and he won't rest. They aren't a foolproof way to keep him safe. A few times he's rubbed his wrists on the guards and hurt himself that way. Brenna lets me make a judgment call, depending on how Mark is feeling that evening.

Sometimes she overrules me.

Tonight I didn't put them on. After what happened earlier, I thought binding him to the bed would only make him worse, and give him a sense of claustrophobia.

But now I wish I had.

He's sprawled on the floor. There are random alarms coming from sensors that are detached and machines disconnected from my patient.

"Why didn't you use the intercom?" I ask Brenna. I can't believe she left him like this to get me.

"I did," Brenna tells me through gritted teeth. She's bent over her husband, trying to press the palms of her hands down onto his shoulders and whispering soothing sounds under her breath. "You didn't answer."

Because I was standing outside her children's rooms, I think.

"Did something happen?" I run across the room to our medical supplies cabinet, and search for the strongest sedative we have and a fresh needle to push through Mark's IV, which is thankfully still attached.

Mark doesn't seem to be soothed by Brenna's presence, and despite her efforts he continues to thrash his arms and legs. His eyes are wide open and blank with terror.

"They were here," he insists, and a small spray of spit flies from his mouth and lands on Brenna's face. She bends her neck to wipe her face on her shoulder, keeping her hands on her husband's like she's offering some sort of prayer through her touch.

Please let him be okay.

"Nobody was here, my love. I was right in the other room. Nobody can get in. You're safe," she tells him, trying to move her eyes to meet his. "You're safe."

But Mark only looks through her.

I prep the injection, calculating the dosage to account for the sleeping pills I gave him earlier tonight, and push it into his IV. It only takes about twenty seconds for his pounding heart to work the medication through his body.

Finally, he goes limp underneath Brenna's touch and his eyes close.

"Help me move him back to bed," Brenna says.

She grips at his shoulders, and I take his feet. Mark's heavy as a corpse as we move him back into bed. Without having to say a word to each other, we both silently fasten the straps around his wrists and ankles.

For his own protection, I tell myself.

7

DAY 2

TOBIAS

Jasmine stares me down with those huge brown eyes of hers, and I find myself meekly ducking my head behind a beam in the stables to break our eye contact. I know she's just a horse—of course I know that—but sometimes it feels like they're able to read me better than actual people can.

Julie whickers in her stall opposite Jasmine, and I decide a brush down would be a welcome distraction. I learned a long time ago that you have to accept the things you can't change, and I can't change anything about being locked down at Granfield for the foreseeable future. I can't change the fact that I went to check on Mark right after the alert came across my phone, or that I let him convince me in that way he has to carry him out of his bed and onto the balcony closest to his rooms.

"I want to see the sky," he told me.

The brushes fit perfectly into my hands, and the leather strap that circles around my palm is worn from years of good use.

I take Jasmine out first, starting on her right shoulder and moving along her flank, and then on to her left side. She's stoic, staring out into the field beyond the stables. I slept deeply last night. So deeply that I woke up in the morning and had to pause for a second to remember where I was, and what I needed to do. I thought the adrenaline pumping through my body, urging me to take off running into the woods, would keep me up.

But it didn't.

I could never leave anyway. No one else besides Mark really knows how to take care of the horses, and he can't anymore. All they have is me now.

Brenna would come to ride them, sometimes, but she never showed any interest beyond getting up and down from the saddle. She always left the clean-up for me, which is fine. That's my job, after all. Daphne seems to be really curious about them, but she won't ride them yet. She's still a little too nervous to climb up, even onto Julie, who's used to taking orders from Jasmine, and so she translates that into being the gentlest to ride.

I work my way back to Jasmine's mane, which I always leave for last. As I move forward, though, her ears pin back against her head.

Someone else is outside.

"Hello," I call out. There's a wind that's kicked up, and a gust brings a swirl of dead leaves whipping through the entranceway. The scratching of the leaves is surprisingly loud and it's all I can hear for a few seconds, but Jasmine is still on alert. I glance over at Julie, and she's equally tense, with her long face pulled down and her eyes shifting from Jasmine to the open stable door.

"Hello," I say again, trying to push my voice against the strengthening wind. A storm is probably coming.

There's a crunch of gravel outside, and a moment later Darren appears with a sharp rake in hand and sweat dripping off his forehead despite the cooler weather.

"Morning," he says, and tips his head towards me.

Darren was out running errands in town when the lockdown

order came. After the governor closed down the roads for all but essential services, Darren said he had a hell of a time getting back to Granfield. He said the roads were blockaded with police and that they wouldn't let him pass at first, until he was able to prove that he worked at Granfield.

He stumbles a bit when he takes a step into the stable, and his rake goes clattering down to the ground.

"Sorry about that. I've been working out in the north-facing flower beds, trying to prep them for spring. I got a little carried away, I guess." He shrugs and bends to sit down on an upturned bucket. "Those yew bushes can be tough to wrangle back."

I don't say anything to him, because my mind is busy ticking off what the news has been telling us, in more and more rapid rotation, for the last month. Symptoms include: Dry cough. Shortness of breath. Fever.

Darren stares at his hands. Even from where I'm standing I can see they're shaking. He glances up and catches me looking, and then shoves his hands into his pockets.

I haven't been into town for at least a few weeks. We order feed for the horses online, and it gets delivered every month by a father-daughter team driving a white van. Mark had insisted we feed them only organic oats and hay, although sometimes I slip them a few cubes of Domino brand sugar, which I also put in my coffee in the mornings.

Can horses get sick with it too?

I try to push the thought away, but it needles at me.

"How are you feeling?" I ask him. "Maybe you should go rest."

I try to make my voice more commanding than usual, but Darren doesn't take the hint.

"I have a lot more work to do. Spring is always a busy time for Granfield."

"I suppose that's a silver-lining from this entire mess." I call this over my shoulder as I start to lead Jasmine back to her stall, and farther away from Darren. "All we have now is time."

Darren gives a grunt that turns into a cough.

Jasmine stops moving, and I have to put my hand flat against her side and guide her in through the stall door.

I'm trying to think about what to do.

The news said there's a three percent death rate for this new virus. Which doesn't seem too extreme, until you hear the other statistic.

For people with other health conditions, like immune disorders or respiratory problems, then the mortality jumps to around thirty percent.

And we don't know whether the sickness can travel from species to species. We don't know whether it kills horses like it kills people.

"Your girl there seems to be feisty today." Darren's voice clips off at the end of the sentence, and another cough rattles through his chest.

I look over my shoulder, and he's still sitting on that bucket at the front of the stables. He's conscious, but barely it seems. Darren's eyes flit from spot to spot, like Julie's were a few minutes ago, right before Darren showed up.

Jasmine's sleeping blanket flipped over her stall. I give myself a few seconds to consider it. It's heavy, and thick enough to keep a big animal warm through winter nights. It could stop a man from breathing.

I'd have to burn the blanket afterwards.

"Darren," I begin to say, reaching out for the blanket. Letting my mind go where it needs to go, and pushing the black hole that's opened in my stomach down as far as it will go. I run through my head the list of places Darren has been, the things he's touched.

I'll have to burn all of those too.

The blanket is rough under my fingertips, and I have to tense my shoulder as I pull it down from its resting place on the boards surrounding Jasmine. She's quiet in her stall. Julie looks on silently from behind me.

Like I said, sometimes horses know me better than people do.

I turn my head to the side and take a deep breath through the fabric of my shirt. I hear Darren breathe his own raspy breath. Another coughing fit is bound to start soon.

They keep saying that's how it spreads the fastest. Through droplets that we breathe in from someone else.

It has to be now.

I take the blanket in both hands and tense my chest, ready to wrap Darren's head and upper body in it and roll him to the ground and out into the fields beyond. I know I'll have to put extra pressure on the top of the blanket, to get him to stop breathing. To stop coughing, and spreading his sickness.

"Hello," a voice says from the open stable doors. It's a small voice. A young voice.

I look up, blanket stretched between my hands, ready to smother the poor landscaper who had the unfortunate luck of going into town.

Daphne's ringlet curls frame her head. She's wearing a bright pink dress today, with strawberries dancing across the fabric.

"Can I pet the horses?" she asks. "I'm so bored."

I don't hesitate. I run over to her, wrap the blanket around her as I pick her up in my arms, and take off towards the main house.

I ignore her protests. She wriggles against my chest, but I keep repeating the same thing, over and over again.

"It's too late," I tell her. "It's too late."

8

FELIX

Daphne and I are in the panic room. She's reading a book with unicorns on the cover and I'm trying to do a crossword puzzle. The walls of the room are so thick that you can't get a wireless signal, so both of us are having to entertain ourselves the old-fashioned way.

We've been in here for almost five hours. My watch is analog still. Dad gave it to me.

Mom's come to check on us a few times already, and her face looms up on the screen, disembodied and ghost-like when we least expect it.

"We're almost done," she tells us each time she jumps in to assure us that everything is perfectly fine. They just need us to stay in there a little longer. And then she says she loves us, but before Daphne or I can respond and tell her we love her too, the screen goes blank and she's gone.

One time at lunch I told the kids at my table that my family had a safe room. I may have called it a panic room, which probably made it even worse. But I was genuinely surprised that these other kids didn't have a room like it in their houses.

"It's for when you need to go to a safe place," I explained to them, like I was our math teacher walking them through an algebra problem.

One boy who was pretty much nice to everyone and who had a port wine birthmark on the side of his right cheek was clearly going to try to make sense of what I was saying.

"You mean, like where you go when there's a tornado? In my house, we go down to the basement and stand in the corner by the washer and dryer."

I go to a fancy school. Parents have to pay a lot of money for their kids to go there, and you have to make an application video and write an essay—most people's parents write them for their kids, I think, although Mom and Dad insisted I write my own. And everyone is really smart and sophisticated and posh. Which is partly why I couldn't understand that this was the reaction I was getting. I'd never even seen the washer and dryer in our house. That was something Greta took care of.

"No. Like a safe room you go to if people are in your house and trying to hurt your family." All the faces seated around the long white cafeteria table stared back at me with confusion or concern, or—worst of all—fear on their faces.

"It has padded walls and a special locking door, and nobody can get in or out without a code. There's even a pad that scans your eye, like in the movies."

Total disbelief. A few of them started looking around the room for an excuse to get up. The nice boy with the red cheek gathered up the trash at the table and stood to throw it away in the communal trash bin.

"That sounds weird," a small boy with freckles and a cowlick said. "Your family is weird."

To their credit, none of the other boys laughed with him.

After that, I started eating lunch in the library behind the 570.35-570.59 shelf. I also broke into Freckle's locker and put a heavy dose of clear liquid laxative into the bread of his sandwich.

I never got caught.

I was upstairs in the old nanny's rooms, staring through my telescope when I spotted Tobias hauling a huge blanket with tiny legs and arms wriggling out of it across the lawn at a full sprint. It took me a second to realize he had Daphne wrapped up in his arms. I blinked my lashes against the glass lens and tried to refocus my eyes. But what I saw was still the same. Tobias' mouth was open like he was howling into the air. I'd never seen a grown-up look terrified before.

I couldn't see Daphne's face.

I rushed from the attic rooms and down the shallower wood stairs from third to second floor, and then on down the plushier stairs that take you from the second to the first floor. I was going to stay quiet and composed, like you see heroes do in action movies when faced with a crisis, but the sounds spilled out of my mouth, louder the closer I got to where I knew I'd cross with Tobias and my sister.

"Help," I screamed, until I was sucking in air and barely choking out the words. "Help them!"

Margot got there first. "What's happening?" She put her hands on my shoulders and stared into my eyes. I had to fight the urge to wriggle away from her touching me and keep running.

I started to explain what I'd seen, but Tobias made it to the main house before I could finish. There was a loud banging on the back door, where the kitchen leads out onto the patio, and Margot let go of me long enough that I was able to slip from her grasp and open the door. Tobias didn't look at either of us. He strode in, putting Daphne on the ground and releasing the blanket from around her.

"Darren is sick," he told the shining kitchen tiles. "He's in the stables right now. I need to go back and take care of him."

Margot was helping Daphne untangle herself from the blanket. "I'll go help you."

"No!" It was my mother's voice. She stood at the entrance to the kitchen, backlit by the light streaming in through the windows in the main hall. Her hands were behind her back, like she was hiding something. I don't know how long she'd been there.

I hadn't seen her the entire day. She was wearing jeans and a stretched-out sweatshirt, and her hair poked out from around her. She looked like a faded copy of her normal self.

"Margot, take the children to the safe room." Mom never called it the panic room in front of us, although I'd often heard her say that's what it actually was, while she was hiring people to build it after everything that happened with Dad. She was still standing in the doorway. I thought it was weird that she wouldn't go near us, because usually she was trying to hug us or kiss the tops of our heads whenever she was actually home. Mom turned to Tobias, who had the blanket gripped in his hands so tight his knuckles were white. "I'll go with you."

Margot cast a sidelong look at my mother, but she didn't say anything. Silently, she reached out and took Daphne's hand and started to walk away from the rest of us. When I paused for a second, my mother's voice cut through the air sharp like a knife. "Go," she said, so I slunk off to join my sister while the grown-ups took care of Darren.

Margot hadn't stayed with us in the safe room. She said she'd be back to check on us, but that she needed to help our Mom and that, since she was a nurse, they needed her especially.

"What do you think they're doing?" Daphne's voice breaks into my thoughts.

"They're trying to figure out what's wrong with Darren."

She turns a page in her book. My sister doesn't look up from the colorful drawings of horses with pink tails and starbursts on their flanks. "They know what's wrong with him."

I try to ignore her. Sometimes my sister can be difficult.

I read the next clue in the crossword puzzle. Five across. Seven letters. A reptile from South America.

"I *said*, they already know what's wrong with him. That's why we're in here."

Daphne sets her book down, and stares over at me from beneath a curtain of her blond curls. "I saw him, you know. I was at the stables."

"What were you doing out there by yourself?" She's not allowed by the horses without an adult chaperoning her. She knows that.

"I just wanted to see them. But before I could get in and pet them, there was all this coughing and Tobias was saying something to Darren I think and then, boom, he'd grabbed me and carried me to the house in that blanket that smelled like hay and old wood."

"Do you want to play a game?" I ask my sister, hoping to distract her from what I think she's about to say, but it doesn't work.

"They're going to kill him, you know," Daphne says, before she tilts her head back to her book. She flips another page. "That's why we're locked in here. Because he has to die."

9

DAY 3
BRENNA

It's not yet dawn. The tile of the floor beneath my bare feet is freezing from the night air. Mark had wanted to put in heated tiles, but I wouldn't let him. I told him it was too pampered a life. What kind of children would we raise if they never had to experience any sort of discomfort, I'd asked him.

He'd only raised his eyebrow and deferred to me with a deep kiss and a squeeze of my shoulder. We were years away from having children, but even then we knew.

Or, at least we thought we did.

I flick on the recessed lights above the sink in the kitchen and start to make a list.

Outside the kitchen window there's a thick fog that's come to lay around the small hills and valleys of the surrounding fields. I wonder if the horses are warm inside their stable. If Jasmine is missing her blanket.

I fight the violent, rapid urge to vomit. I don't have time for this.

I grip my pen and write down what I know.

We definitely don't have enough cereal. Or milk. I wish I'd had Greta stock up on things like peanut butter, with lots of protein and fat. Something growing bodies could really depend on. Daphne loved having peanut butter on toast in the morning for her breakfast.

But Margot's allergic to peanuts.

We don't have enough of a lot of things.

I scan the cupboards of the sleek Swedish-inspired shelving Mark had installed when we first moved in. They are bursting in certain areas, with bags of lentils and quinoa almost overflowing from the clear edges designed to hold everything in without seeming obtrusive. All the chalkboard labels are written in somebody else's handwriting—probably Greta's. Or one of the other people we paid to help make this huge house run.

There's somehow only one bag of coffee beans left. And our labeled Pasta (GF) has a single sad bag of corkscrew pieces made from brown rice. I'd had the bright idea a little while ago that gluten might be bad for us, and so anything with a starchy stable shelf life seems to have been cycled out of Greta's shopping routine for the most part.

The fridge is well stocked for now, because Greta went to the store before she left to be with her mother. There are prepped cuttings of various green vegetables, and a huge bag of chopped kale mixed with collard greens. Two cartons of soy milk and a gallon of normal milk. Cheese, cold cuts, kombuchas and yogurts and two dozen eggs.

And there's the garden, I remind myself.

It's still dark outside, but a skein of light is starting to shade the edges of the pathways and trees. I look down at my list. It seems terribly meagre, considering we are alone out here for an indeterminate amount of time.

And not only alone. Quarantined. Or we would be, if anyone found out that Darren was sick.

I push the thought away and slip on a pair of shoes left by the door and pull an old wax coat hanging on a hook. I freeze for a second after I pull my arms through the sleeves, thinking that it must be Darren's. That I'm infected now too. That I won't be able to touch my children again. Or my husband.

Or Margot.

I force myself to take a breath, and shrug against the stiff fabric. It fits perfectly. The sleeves hit at my wrists, with a slight nip in the waist. This is a woman's jacket.

Darren wouldn't have left his jacket here. Greta didn't like him, to the point that I had to have a little talk with her a while back about everyone at Granfield being part of a family and needing to be kind to each other. She gave me a steely stare when I was finished, but things had gotten better after that. Still, there's no way she would have welcomed him in for a chat and some warm scones.

It must be a jacket I forgot I had. Or Margot's, maybe?

It doesn't matter. As long as it's not Darren's.

Fever-ridden and glassy-eyed, his face swims up in front of me like an unwelcome guest.

He didn't recognize me when Tobias and I came for him, I'm at least certain of that.

The shoes slip off the backs of my bare feet as I walk from the kitchen door over to the greenhouse. I'm hoping that things are further along than I'd guess for this time of year.

Maybe Tobias knows something about growing things, because I don't.

My phone pings inside the pocket of my pajama top, where I slipped it in when I got up from the couch outside Mark's room. I tried to do some work, but the words on my laptop screen blurred in front of me. Everything will have to wait for now. He was asleep when I left.

We made the children sleep in the panic room, and I have more cleaning to do before they can come out. Margot promised she would help.

I pull my phone out and scan the series of messages coming in almost constantly. Since the lockdown order came I've been flooded with more and more frantic texts and emails from my staff, from my board, from investors. I've replied to a few of them, but I'm waiting a little longer before I respond to the rest.

Chronos handles video conferencing tech, and it is going to come out of this pandemic just fine, I'll tell them. People need us now more than ever.

I let my eyes stay for a beat longer on the screen. There's one message directed to me from Mark's former business partner. It came in at 3am. I'll have to read it later.

There's a small light out in the distance, more focused than the diffused glow of the coming dawn. It's coming from Tobias' apartment. I guess I'm not the only one who can't sleep.

There's so much to do.

I walk through the copse of trees that separates the main house from the gardens and greenhouse. On the air is the faint smell of charred wood and something else, more acrid and pungent. It's a smell I remember from my childhood. I hope the wind carries it away from the house, because it's not a smell any child should remember.

I don't see any light from where we set the fire across the hill, which means everything must have burned down by now.

Granfield Manor has a huge greenhouse on the side of the property, close by but out of view of the main house thanks to a copse of ancient ash trees that grow along the furthest edge of the lake. The greenhouse was originally meant to grow orchids, but over the years it was converted into a hothouse for edible plants, with a seasonal garden carved out of the earth around it when the growing season began outside. It was in some disrepair when Mark and I first moved in, but we hired Darren and then Darren hired a team and it became something else. We'd apparently won a few blue ribbons at the county fair.

I trip on a root spanning across the pathway and fall down onto my hands and knees. A few small rocks cut into the soft flesh of my palms, and the list I've brought with me crumples against the hard ground. I should have brought a flashlight.

How am I going to make a list of all the plants if I can't even see where they are?

I scramble back up and move ahead again, not willing to waste the battery on my phone with its light turned on. I need to be more careful, moving through the dark.

Finally, the path turns and I come out of the grouping of trees into a clearing. The ghostly structure of the greenhouse looms up ahead of me, like Miss Havisham waiting in her wedding dress. The ground around it is loamy and recently turned—I can smell the deep richness of the dirt. It smells like springtime, but a hundred times more powerful.

I reach the door to the greenhouse and slip on one of the plastic gloves from Mark's medical supplies. Tobias had difficulty fitting his hands into them last night, because I've only ever ordered smalls or mediums. It's only ever been women taking care of Mark. Tobias will just have to make them work, and stretch them out so they'll fit.

Inside the greenhouse, there are rows and rows of tables covered in small green plants. It's too dark to discern the starts sprouting in their tiny plastic and cardboard containers, and even if I had good lighting I wouldn't know enough to identify anything beyond a tomato plant. I grip the list I'm making for Tobias and Margot of what we'll have to eat for the next month. Months.

I won't go further than that when I talk to them.

I won't bring up the possibility of years. It's too much to handle, for all of us.

10

MARGOT

If I'd gone to be with Darren, I wouldn't be here with Mark. Brenna would never allow it.

And I need to be here with Mark. It's the entire reason I came to Granfield in the first place. I couldn't risk losing everything now, even if it meant that I couldn't look myself in the eye this morning when I stood in front of the mirror and brushed my teeth, washed my face like it was any other morning, even though nothing could be further from the truth.

I know they killed Darren. I'm not stupid. And there's a small part of me that's glad I didn't need to be there and become a part of it, more than I already am a part of it by not doing anything. If I'd been there, monitoring him and assessing his symptoms to see how far along he was, I would have felt the need to stop Tobias and Brenna.

And then maybe they would have done the same thing to me, days or weeks later, when I got sick.

I don't remember when I started talking to Mark. It must have been at least a few weeks after I came to Granfield Manor. Maybe more. It was lonelier than I thought it would be, and I couldn't seem to quiet my mind at night. And then, in the mornings, I'd drag myself out of bed and go to Mark's rooms to care for him. Take his blood pressure, check his pulse, give him his medications. Bathe him to prevent bed sores. I'd dress him in the soft cashmere or silk pajamas that lined his closet, depending on how chilled the room felt that morning, and then we'd have time to sit together.

Brenna was already at the office. The children were at school. And Greta or the other staff wouldn't come in unless I let them in to clean. I was one of the few people who had a key card for this portion of the house.

Tobias has one, although I can't really understand why except that Mark wanted him to have it. Sometimes the noises of Mark's monitors would drown out the beeps and other signals that the doors were opening, and Tobias would appear behind me with that hangdog expression of his, like he'd just heard the world was ending or they'd discontinued his favorite horse feed or something. I was never sure how much he overheard before he let me know he was there, but he never asked me about any of it and Brenna never brought it up, so maybe he didn't hear anything.

Today, the house is quiet even though it's after 8am. I know the children are still in the panic room, comfortable and hopefully asleep. Brenna didn't want them coming out yet, not until we'd sanitized everything again. After last night I can't smell anything other than bleach. The house reeks of it because Brenna and I spent most of yesterday scrubbing everything— handles, switches, counters and railings. Anything that Darren might have touched if he'd happened to come inside at some point.

Then we went outside to the shed where Darren kept his tools, and started spraying. We had masks from the medical supplies in Mark's rooms, and gloves too. There was even a stack of gowns that Brenna had bought a while ago. We burned everything afterwards.

We didn't touch Darren's apartment. Instead, Tobias went over and locked the door from the outside, so nobody could get in and somehow get exposed.

We'll have to put on new equipment today for the second and third rounds Brenna said she wants to do. But for now, I'm sitting with Mark, holding his hand and tracing the edges of the white bandage I taped over the long vertical cut on his wrist. I checked it this morning and changed the bandage. It's healing nicely. It'll barely leave a scar by the time all is said and done.

"There's a sickness spreading outside," I tell Mark, although he's not fully awake yet because the extra doses of sedative we've been giving him to help him sleep at night take a while to wear off in the morning. His arms and legs are free, thank God.

Mark was calm and lucid yesterday, despite the panic saturating the house. I hope it means we did a good job pretending in front of him. He told a few jokes, and even with the speech distortions and the motor control of his mouth degrading, I could tell what the punchline was.

"A horse walks into a bar, and the bartender asks, 'Why the long face?'"

For being such a tech wizard, he has really lame jokes.

Brenna and I already agreed to not say anything about Darren, or about the children staying in the panic room. He might be able to smell the bleach on me when he wakes, but we'll see if he asks about it. I've come in here smelling of lots of different things—cold winter wind from a walk out near the horse barns, spicy chilies from a dish Greta was trying out in the kitchen, his wife's perfume on the nape of my neck and down my collarbone. I don't know if the disease is affecting his sense of smell.

Mark stirs a little as I keep talking.

"Brenna was worried it was here. We had a pretty big scare last night. We had to burn a lot of things."

There's a soft rustle as the heater kicks on, and warm air flows from the vent in the upper right corner of the room.

"When I became a nurse, I did it because I wanted to help people." Mark's arm moves a little underneath my fingertips, a twitch of active nerve cells signaling from his brain, and I press a little harder to hopefully give a reassuring pressure on his skin. "I've taken care of people my entire life. I'm good at it."

My mother always wanted me to be a nurse. Sometimes I wonder if that's where her problems came from—that maybe she justified all her weaknesses as a way of giving her daughters practice for the world outside our home.

Mark's eyes flutter open and he immediately locks his gaze onto mine. His eyes are still so piercingly blue, like I saw in those first magazine spreads. There's a powerful man behind all these tubes and machines. I need to remember that.

"Good morning," he tells me. His mouth sounds dry, and I bring over a waiting glass of water for him to sip.

"Better?" I ask.

He licks his lips, which are only slightly cracked. I put some ointment on my finger and dab it onto his lower lip, so he can rub his lips together and spread it around.

"How are you?" This is his standard question, but today it unnerves me and I have to turn and pretend to busy myself with the stand of gauze pads at the other end of the room.

I blink back a few tears, and take a deep breath that I hope he doesn't hear over the soft rustle of the heating above us. I wish for a machine to kick on and start filling the room with its noisy static.

When I turn back, he's not looking at me. His gaze is on the window, where a beam of light has burst through the clouds and streamed in to make a long rectangle of sunshine on the tiles near the entrance to the bathroom.

"It's going to be a beautiful day," he tells me.

I nod. There's a beep from the other room as the keypad allows someone else inside this small sanctuary I've tried to build between us.

"Of course it will be," I tell him.

11

TOBIAS

"What are you thinking about?" Colleen asks me. She's on the beach where we went for our honeymoon in Jamaica. The sand is a white so bright that it seems to vibrate when you look at it.

"You," I say, because it's the truth. All I can think about is her.

She smiles, and her dark hair falls in front of her eyes as she dips her head towards her chest in that bashful way she has. "But what else?"

"What else, what?" I ask her back, teasing a little. She likes it when I tease her.

"You can't just be thinking about me. There has to be something else going through your head."

"Why?"

"Because you looked worried, a moment ago." We'd loved each other a long time. My wife knew me better than anyone. Ever.

"Did I?" I reach out to stroke her face, but my hand falls through the image of her and I'm left with an empty grip. I flex my hand.

No, not an empty grip. I'm holding a shoe—not even a shoe, a boot with laces and a reinforced steel toe, the kind Darren would wear when he was working on the gardens—tight enough to make my knuckles pop up white as the sand. Colleen isn't there anymore. Instead, next to me on the beach is a huge fire, the flames so tall they're licking at the stars in the now-dark sky. I turn around, hoping to see her again. But there's only darkness around me, outside of the fire's light. Until a face looms over me, from out of the deep black of the ocean lapping close enough to spray my bare legs with saltwater.

Bloodshot eyes. Red, pulpy skin pricked with beads of sweat.

"Please," Darren says, even though by the time Brenna and I got to him he wasn't able to speak between his coughs. His mouth could only open into a silent scream that neither of us knew how to care for. "Please don't hurt me."

I shoot up from the couch in my apartment, my body aching from falling asleep in the early morning after hours spent pacing and waiting for the bonfire to burn down. My shoulders ache from dragging the wood and tools into the fire pit. Brenna had been insistent. Everything we could get to that Darren may have touched, outside of his apartment, needed to be burned.

She kept Margot inside the house, rubbing down every surface with bleach.

"Don't let Brenna fool you," Mark had told me once, when we'd been chatting by the stables and I'd mentioned that he must feel really lucky to be married to such a kind and confident —I didn't mention beautiful, because that was obvious to anyone who met her—woman. "She's a killer."

He'd smiled, and I'd figured he was talking about her business life. I knew she ran some sort of tech company, but different from what Mark did. They were both ridiculously successful and wealthy.

Maybe if she'd let Margot come and look at Darren, assess

how sick he was and what we could do to help him. Maybe things would have been different.

Light streams through the windows in my small living room. It must be mid-morning by now, meaning that I slept for at least a few hours.

My mouth feels fuzzy from the shots of whiskey I downed close to 3am, hoping to ease into some artificial calm. I wash my face in the tiny bathroom and run a toothbrush over my teeth. Indigestion burns up my throat from having only a few ounces of hard liquor in my stomach for the twenty-four hours or so.

There's a tightness in my chest that I ignore. We were very, very careful, I remind myself.

I pull on a fresh shirt and rush out the door, realizing that Jasmine and Julie and all their friends must be anxious with hunger. My apartment is only a few yards from the stables, situated over the old mill barn. The manor used to grind its own flour, out at the mill-house near the dam on the edge of the lake. A few old mill wheels are still scattered inside, and their round hulks sometimes loom out from behind the windows like deformed ghosts, waiting for someone to finally let them out of their misery.

The stable door is closed, which is a relief. In the haze of yesterday's emergency, I couldn't remember whether I'd closed it or not. I'm certain I fed the horses dinner, but a glance at my watch tells me it's later than I thought and I'm well behind schedule for their normal breakfast.

When I open the door, I'm met with soft familiar smells. Hay, weathering lumber, and the exhales of large animals waiting to be cared for.

"I'm coming," I assure them in tones meant for babies and horses.

My dream from this morning creeps back into my thoughts.

Colleen and I were going to have a baby. She was five months along, starting to show.

I put the bucket of oats into Jasmine's stall, and she nuzzles my arm with her soft velvet nose. Her ears are tipped forward, and her nostrils flare as she eats.

"You're right, girl," I tell her. "But we've got everything figured out. Everyone's going to be fine."

I move along to Julie, and then to the other horses. A few minutes later, the stable is full of the sounds of large flat teeth grinding down the mixture of hay and oats I like to feed them in the morning. I freshen their water next, make sure to keep my eyes away from the spot where Darren sat yesterday, or the empty spot on the floor where Brenna and I snatched everything he'd touched in order to throw them into the fire.

There's no blood to clean up.

The news says that the disease doesn't travel by blood anyway.

It moves through the air, like a song.

I take Jasmine out to brush down, and feed her a cube of sugar from the palm of my hand. There are only maybe twenty or so left in the box.

As I comb Jasmine's mane into a high shine, I stare out into the field where the creature moved through the tall grass two days ago.

We were going to find out the next week if it was a boy or a girl.

I didn't know until I was in court, and the prosecutor was giving her opening statements. That's when I learned we were having a girl. The coroner was able to tell after doing the autopsy.

The baby would be six now, if she had lived.

Colleen would be thirty-two.

12

FELIX

"Why are they making us stay in here so long?" Daphne's voice has that whiny quality that tells me she's about two seconds away from an all-out tantrum.

They used to be worse when she was younger. She'd kick and scream and bite whoever was nearest to her when she didn't get her way. But then Mom and Dad had somebody with a clipboard and a tight bun come to the house for a few weeks and things got better. I wasn't allowed to be there for whatever they were doing with Daphne though. Mom said it would make her embarrassed.

Mom told me they'd do the same thing for me when she scheduled sessions to help with what has been happening at school. Daphne wouldn't be allowed to watch, or even meet the person who came to help. But then we had to stay home, and school was canceled. We all have bigger problems now, I guess.

We spent the night in the panic room, Daphne and I, and even though there are huge air ducts in the ceiling that supposedly pump fresh air in on a regular basis from some special source, the air smells stale. Like potato chips and jelly sandwiches, which is what we had for dinner last night from the rations stashed away in a pantry drawer in the corner, and morning breath and a slight whiff of chemical toilet from the bathroom.

I'm pretty sure both Daphne and I are a bit dehydrated. It's easy enough to forget to drink water when your normal schedule is disrupted. I read once in a physiology and anatomy book what happens to the human body when it's deprived of enough water.

I don't answer Daphne and instead get up and move to the bathroom to pour a big glass of water. I take a long deep sip and then refill it and bring it over to my sister.

She pushes the cup away from me and turns her shoulders so she's staring into the corner, which is all white padding and clean metal lines.

"You'll feel better if you take a sip."

"How do you think they killed him?" she asks me. I ignore her again, and sit down next to her along the bench. I dare for a second to put my arm around her, like I've seen big brothers do in movies, but when she squirms away I let my arm drop back to my side.

"They didn't kill him." I put the cup down on the bench between us, like a dividing cubicle. I'm still hoping she'll drink it.

By this point, from the white bread and the potato chips, her cells are probably contracting, searching out water from wherever they can find it. She'll be getting a headache soon, if she doesn't have one already.

"Are we going to get sick?"

"That's why Mom has us waiting in here. So we don't get sick."

"Yeah, but I saw him. I was there in the stables with Tobias. He might have coughed on me. He might have *inflicted* me."

"Infected." Realizing my mistake, I add, "He didn't infect you.

You're fine. You said you didn't get close to him, and Tobias wrapped you up in that blanket and carried you to the house to be extra safe. And then Mom made us wait up in here. So you're fine, and I'm fine."

I nod reassuringly, but Daphne can't see because her head is still turned away.

I nudge the glass of water closer to her leg.

"I want Mom," she says.

"Me too."

We haven't seen our mother since yesterday evening, although she might have popped in on the video screen to check on us while we were sleeping. It was surprising how easy it was to fall asleep, even though the cots in the panic room are tinier than my normal bed and the pillows are scratchier. Daphne was asleep almost as soon as her head hit the pillow.

The only issue is that you can't turn the lights off in the room. They stay on, in case of emergency. So that was a little weird, but there were eye masks under each of the pillows that Daphne and I could use. Mom reminded us about them when she came to say goodnight.

She looked stretched out in the video monitor when we last saw her. It was like her neck and shoulders were pulling away from each other. I'd read about cheekbones and bone structure in that same anatomy book where they talked about the effects of dehydration, but I'd never really noticed anybody's cheekbones until I saw my mother on that screen last night. They were like two knives, slicing across her face and making the shadows in her cheeks darker.

I hope Mom got some sleep last night too. I know she's doing all of this for us.

And for Dad.

"Do you want to play a game?"

Daphne shrugs, but I see her right arm slip out from

underneath where she's tucked it against her chest and grasp out for the glass of water.

She takes a sip. And then another.

"What should we play?" she asks meekly, and internally I take a deep sigh because I think we've passed the danger zone, and because she's doing what I asked her to do.

"What do you want to play?"

"Hide and seek," she answers immediately.

I look around our surroundings. Four walls with four cots built into the one side. A pantry shelf full of food, and the door that leads into the bathroom.

"There's not really anywhere to hide," I say cautiously.

"But that's what I want to play!" That edge to her voice is back.

Daphne stands up and balls her hands into two little fists. "Please, Felix. Please, please pretty please!"

"But where would we hide?" I try to reason with her.

A crimson flush spreads over her neck and cheeks. "I want to hide from everyone!" she shouts. "I don't want to be here anymore! I'm sick of being stuck inside here with *you*!"

I hold out my hands, palms flat, in a sign of calm or surrender—I figure either will work at the moment.

"Okay, okay, we can play hide and seek. Which do you want to do first?"

But it's too late. I've seen this happen too many times. She has to ride this out, and then she'll collapse in an exhausted heap, all of her energy spent.

"I said, I don't want to be here with you anymore!" Daphne's eyes bug out of her face as she shouts at me. "I hate you. You are the worst, ugliest, stupidest, most disgusting brother in the world."

I grit my teeth. I know she doesn't mean any of this.

It's just hard to remember sometimes, when your sister's spit is flying in your face and your father is dying and your mother has forced you into the panic room in your haunted mansion because somebody has brought a deadly infectious disease into your quarantined house.

"It's going to be all right," I say in as soothing a voice as I can manage. My arms are still held out, and they're serving as a shield to Daphne's flailing arms and legs while her tantrum hits its crescendo—we'd just started to pick out instruments in school before all of this happened. I was going to play the saxophone.

"No, nothing is ever going to be all right, ever again. Not until I don't have such an awful, stupid, ugly brother." She pauses for a second, and every rational part of my brain knows she's going to try to hurt me as much as possible, and even still I can't control my reaction to what she says next.

"No wonder everyone at school hates you. No wonder you don't have any friends. Even Mom and Dad have to pretend to like you. Why don't you just die already, because no one would care if you were here or not."

I reach out and slap her hard across the face. So hard that one of her baby teeth—which was loose already, but still—flies out from her mouth, along with an arc of blood and spit. It leaves a streak of red along one of the white padded walls.

"Shut your mouth, you stupid bitch," I tell her, and instantly regret it. I instantly regret everything that happened in the last two seconds.

"Felix," a voice echoes from the locked doorway of the room, panic and rage stretching the words out. "What are you doing?"

I don't have to turn my head from my sister's bleeding mouth. I already know.

It's Mom, come to save us both.

13

DAY 4
BRENNA

I wake first. Before I can stop myself, I brush a tendril of hair back from her forehead.

Margot's eyes flutter open, and she gives me a sleepy smile.

I force my mouth into something that resembles a smile, because she deserves it. She's not the reason for the sharp pains threatening to rip open my body, straight down the middle until I don't have to feel anything anymore.

"I missed you."

Margot looks away as she says this to me, shyness getting the better of her. She's sprawled across the bed, naked from the waist up. Her dark hair falls along her shoulders in loose curls and there's a red flush spread under her right collarbone that I touch with my fingertips, like a baker testing to see if their tender cake is done. My fingers leave a small white circle before the flush spreads back across Margot's skin. I bend down to kiss her, and as I do Margot reaches her hands from inside the bedsheets and runs her fingers through my hair, which I can feel is damp from sweating in my sleep.

It's not a crime to be lonely, I remind myself.

She's a kind person. Margot.

Kindness can be its own aphrodisiac. Sometimes it's better than beauty—although Margot is objectively gorgeous, with her dark brown eyes and rich chestnut hair framing a face straight out of some Renaissance portrait. And better than strength—although I've seen Margot clean the gaping wounds my husband gives himself, and change his soiled sheets, and yesterday I saw her take a deep breath and move forward with the danger at hand like a soldier going into battle; there's nothing about her that doesn't seem to be reinforced with steel underneath.

When someone is kind to you, you know that you matter in this world, if only for the sake of being able to make that person feel better about themselves because they're caring for you in that moment.

After finding my children ready to kill each other in the one place I thought they'd stay safe, I felt so useless.

So I went to find Margot last night, after the children were back in their own beds.

We didn't say a word to each other. I kissed her, and she pulled the door closed behind me and now here we are, with the morning light arcing through her bedroom windows onto her porcelain skin.

I pull my sweater from yesterday back over my head, and the cashmere slips over the welts on my shoulders like a gentle caress. Bruises are popping up on my body in unexpected places, and I'm certain I don't want Margot to see them any more than she already has.

"Where are you going?" she asks me as I stand.

"The children will be waking soon." I scan the room for anything else I might have scattered onto the floor last night. I see the clip for my hair underneath the armchair in the corner, and bend down to snatch it up. "I don't want them to wake to an empty house."

Margot nods and gets up from the bed. "Okay. I'll start on breakfast."

But I suddenly don't want her there, reeking of sex and our night together as she cooks eggs for my children.

"That's okay." I force a smile again. She doesn't deserve this, but I'm doing it all the same. "I can handle that. Why don't you go and check on Mark, and then we can trade?"

"I'm sorry about Darren."

I'd turned towards the door, my hand poised on the handle and ready to make my quick escape, but she knows she's got me again.

"There's nothing to be sorry for. It had to happen. We couldn't risk anyone else getting infected."

I lock my eyes on hers, seeing if she might challenge the rationale I've been playing across the back of my own mind since Tobias shut the door to Darren's apartment and told me that it was finished.

"I know. I'm still sorry."

Margot stands and slips her arms around me. She's only wearing pajama shorts, and I let myself reach out and put my palms flat against the two pale crescents of her shoulder blades. Everything about her is so different from Mark.

I let go, her skin underneath my hands suddenly too hot to touch.

There's a soft groan that echoes from somewhere further inside the house.

My eyes meet Margot's again, and she flashes her eyebrows at me, as if to say, "Don't you know?"

"What was that?" I ask.

She's still so close to me that I can smell the bit of toothpaste on her breath. She must have gotten up in the night to brush her teeth, after I'd fallen asleep despite trying to stay awake, and made it back to the couch in Mark's rooms.

Nervous energy tugs at my legs. I need to go. There's so much to do.

The moan comes again, this time stretching longer across the still air of the house.

"I don't understand," I tell Margot. Nothing about what's happening makes any sense. Nothing about this house is right.

Margot's face softens and she puts her hand up on my shoulder in such a way that I have to fight the urge to swat it off.

"It's Felix. It's your son."

14

FELIX

I woke crying again. I don't know why it happens some mornings and not others.

It's not even really a cry. It's more like a howl—like you'd hear from some mutant in a movie—that comes from deep inside my chest. It knows it doesn't belong inside me, and so it fights to get out.

I haven't told anyone about it, because even though it's scary when it's happening, I feel a lot better afterwards. You know how when you're sick to your stomach, and then you finally throw up whatever bad food you ate, and then suddenly your body gives this sigh of relief and you feel a hundred percent better. That's what it feels like, and if I tell someone about it, then they might do something that makes it stop. And then I'd feel sick forever.

My bedroom is bright with sunshine. I do a quick assessment to try to see if I need to let any more out, but inside my chest is quiet.

There's a peacefulness in my head that comes too, after it's done.

I hear a soft creak outside my door, but when I pause for a moment to see if somebody might be coming in, there's no knock that follows and the hallway goes quiet. It's windy outside, so air is probably seeping into the house through cracks and making it sound like people are going up and down the halls and in and out of rooms.

My telescope is waiting for me in the corner after I climb out of bed and use the bathroom. Sometimes the best sightings I have are in the early morning, when the rest of the world thinks everyone else is still getting up. I point over at the stables, but there's a mist that's fallen onto the valley and I can only make out the roof of the building clearly. I swing the viewer over to the further corner of our property, where the greenhouse sits next to Darren's apartment and the old machinery barn. There's a few swirls of smoke still snaking up from somewhere near the glass walls of the greenhouse, but it's gotten too light to see if there's a fire burning that far away.

Mom said yesterday that Darren had to leave, because he was really sick, and that Daphne and I weren't allowed to go near his apartment. If we did, she said we'd lose our screen time for an entire week, which Daphne and I both know is a bluff on Mom's part. She wouldn't be able to survive with us all gathered inside this house without our screens for distraction. Still, I don't want to worry her, and she seemed really scared by the idea of us going anywhere near his apartment.

I make a note to check on the vectors of viruses in the book I left on my desk. I like looking up information in books rather than on the internet. It's so easy to get overwhelmed online, or to get into stuff that's nasty or nude or both, whereas books have beginnings and ends and only include information that's related to the actual reason the book exists in the first place.

I should know something about viruses and how they spread already, but I don't. Knowledge is power and all that, but I didn't want to look this stuff up, not when it was clear that it was about to happen *to* us.

There's no fog around Darren's apartment, and I refocus the lens of my telescope, hoping to get a closer view of what's inside. I never had much interest in him before this, but now Mom doesn't want me over there I really want to look.

What I see is totally uninteresting. There are the familiar outlines of a sofa and bookcase through one window, and I can see the digital display of what looks like a microwave on a stand through the other window on the side of the building facing towards my room.

I sit back and blink my eye. Sometimes this helps me see better.

When I put my face back against the viewfinder, something shifts inside the apartment. There's a dark shadow that moves from one side to the other, blocking out the green numbers glowing out of the microwave display for a second or two before everything comes back into focus again.

I look over at the next window, hoping to keep track of whatever was moving inside Darren's apartment as it made its path across the space, but I don't see it again.

I've never been inside Darren's place, so I don't know if there's a stairwell in the middle of the building or another way to get in besides the outer door I can see. Whoever was in there might have gone through another door and down the stairs. Or stayed up on the second floor, hidden from the windows for some reason.

I move my telescope so that I'm watching the door of the mill barn. It's the only exit to the building that I can remember from when I've wandered around outside, which I totally admit isn't that often. I'm not really the outdoorsy kind of kid. Whoever or whatever was inside would have to go out that way, I figure.

Unless it was an animal, like a squirrel or a raccoon, that somehow got in.

But what's the likelihood of that, when Mom had said they'd

locked his apartment up tight and they would know if Daphne or I went over there and started messing around.

I look at the door for hours, until I can't sit any longer and my empty stomach tells me I need to go downstairs and eat something. The whole time I'm there, though, nobody comes out the door. The apartment seems to be empty, and I start to believe that what I saw was just a trick of the light.

15

MARGOT

After Brenna leaves I sit for what seems like a long time in bed and stare out into nothing. The sounds from Felix's room have stopped, and I figure Brenna has gone to comfort her son from his bad dream.

She's a good mother. Attentive. Kind. Affectionate.

My skin feels raw from last night. There are a few small abrasions on my thighs and breasts, but they don't hurt so much as pulse under the tight surface of my skin. Tracing the places Brenna touched makes me miss her though.

My mother used to stare out into deep spaces, ignoring my sisters and me as we tried to get her attention. I don't know what she was thinking about when she'd disappear like that. Some days she wouldn't get out of bed.

I jump up and throw on jeans and a sweater, pull my unruly hair back into a ponytail, and wash my face clean and bare, avoiding the mirror affixed directly above the sink. I don't take a shower because I can still smell her on me and it's a welcome distraction from the other thoughts burning through my head. There's no way to know when she might want to be together again, like that. Or even if she will.

I spit into the sink, wipe the extra toothpaste that always spills from the edges of my mouth on a towel, and grab my key card from my bedside table where I keep it at night. I bite down on my tongue hard with my teeth, breathe in through my nose and out through my mouth, and leave my room so that I can give my lover's husband his medicine and a sponge bath.

Lover. It's such a silly word. But Brenna isn't my girlfriend. She's not even really my friend. We're just filling up the empty spaces inside each other. What else do you call that?

I swing through the kitchen on my way to the medical wing so I can grab a quick sip of coffee and one of the energy bars Greta stockpiled in the pantry well before this pandemic. The shelves look emptier than I imagined them, and I think about eating only half a bar and saving the rest for later, but the growl in my stomach insists that I put some energy into my body. I didn't eat much yesterday, or the day before that. I don't have much of an appetite, but the slight tremble in my fingertips tells me otherwise.

Nursing 101. Are your client's basic needs being met? Are they hungry, cold, tired, frightened? What can you do about it?

When I close the pantry door Daphne appears at my side like a little sprite. She doesn't seem affected by a day and a half holed up in the panic room while we disinfected everything, which is good. Kids are so resilient. They can recover from pretty much anything.

"Do you want to have breakfast with me?" she asks, swinging a teddy bear from her hand in a wide arc. I don't recognize the toy, but then again Brenna's kids have more to play with than my sisters and I shared together in our entire childhood.

"I have to go check on your dad." I bite into the protein bar and immediately take a sip of coffee from my mug. The bar feels like sawdust in my mouth, and I need something to wash down the chalky residue. I gag a little trying to get the liquid down my throat.

"Those don't have nuts in them, do they?" Daphne stares at me intently. "Aren't you allergic to nuts?"

I cough and take another sip.

I'd already checked the packaging before taking a bite. Soy and chocolate and coconut, but no actual nuts. Brenna had automatically asked if I had any allergies when I initially came to work for them—apparently Felix had an egg allergy they'd caught only by mistake and a trip to the ER—and it'd been one of our first real conversations when I told her about my family's own scare after I ate a friend's peanut butter sandwich at school and had to be rushed to the hospital.

We were more a bologna and ketchup kind of family. My older sister, Teresa, did most of the grocery shopping, and she hated peanut butter, so she never bought it.

"I'm fine," I assure Daphne, but she keeps staring at me and I wonder if she's scared about something else and just hiding it well. Maybe being in the panic room was scarier for her than I first realized.

I reach out to her, but she moves away and sits down at the kitchen counter in the corner, near the large picture windows and French doors that open onto the patio.

"I can eat whatever I want," she says proudly. She pulls up a chair and settles the teddy bear next to her. "So can teddy."

I watch as Daphne swipes a petite hand across her face and rests her chin in it, her elbow balanced on the edge of the table. She sits there for a few moments, quietly alone, before I get the point.

"Do you need help getting your breakfast?" I finally ask. I glance down at my watch, and figure I have a few minutes still. Mark needs his medications in the morning, but a few minutes here or there on either side won't hurt him.

"Yes, please." A smile crosses Daphne's face, and I feel one of the tight spaces in my chest loosen a little.

I ask her what she'd like, turning towards the fridge and automatically reaching for the milk on the side door.

"Toast and peanut butter, please." She twists towards the teddy bear and leans her head down, as if the toy is whispering in her ear. "Teddy would like some, too."

"I don't think we have peanut butter," I tell her, "but you can definitely have some toast with jelly." Brenna was really insistent to keep her house nut-free after hearing about my allergy. As I swing the door closed though, I ignore the carton of eggs sitting on the top shelf.

"I want peanut butter," Daphne insists, and throws her arms over her chest. "Mommy keeps some in the bottom drawer, with the paper plates and napkins."

"Okay," I say, trying to appease her. Daphne's face has turned bright red over the course of the last several seconds, and I remind myself that everything about this situation that is hard for a grown-up is probably ten times harder for a child.

After pulling a plate from the cupboard and putting two slices of wheat bread into the toaster, I go to the drawer and pull it open. Sure enough, there's a jar of peanut butter nestled in among the rarely used paper plates and plastic cups.

I know my allergy isn't so bad that I can't even touch a peanut, but I still feel a little cautious grabbing at the jar.

The toast pops from the two slots in the toaster and I snatch a butter knife from the cutlery drawer. I need to get over to Mark.

I wonder if Brenna is still with Felix. Maybe she'll be over with her husband by now.

"Here you go." I put the plate of toast down in front of Daphne, along with the jar and knife. I've seen Daphne butter her bread before, and I figure she can do this for herself.

I turn, not really expecting a "thank you" but a little disappointed all the same that Daphne doesn't say anything at first.

"Teddy needs you to do his toast," she calls after me.

"I need to go help your dad," I remind her over my shoulder. My eyes catch hers for a moment, and the change in her face makes me almost stop.

"But Teddy can't do his toast by himself." Daphne's voice becomes a whine, but her face remains furious. I've never seen one of Daphne's tantrums, although one night over a glass of wine Brenna talked about how hard it was to get a therapist to come to the house to help Daphne with her "anger issues".

"I'm sorry," I stammer, not sure exactly what to do. I've already delayed long enough. I need to get over to my patient. "I can come back later and help your Teddy with his toast."

"No," Daphne screams. She jumps up from her chair, knocking over her plate and tipping the jar of peanut butter so it oozes out of the container and onto the table. "I want it now!"

I instinctively start to back away, and bump into something behind me.

"What's going on here?" Brenna says. She looks tired, with deep circles under her eyes that I didn't notice in my room earlier. She still has on the same clothes from yesterday, and her hair has a look of needing to be washed.

Brenna's eyes dart from me to her daughter, and widen as they take in the scene.

"Daphne, where did you get that peanut butter from? Margot is allergic. You know that." She reaches to right the tipped over jar.

It's my turn to glance between Brenna and Daphne. The little girl had known exactly where it was, and she'd said her mom kept it there.

Then Brenna's eyes fall on the teddy bear seated next to Daphne.

"Where did you get that?" Her voice is so quiet that I almost can't hear her. She repeats her question when Daphne doesn't answer, cowering in her seat instead. "Where did you get that bear, Daphne?"

"I don't know," Daphne replies, and she's hunched into a small ball, with her head tucked into her chest and her shoulders folded in, like she's trying to disappear.

Brenna steps over to her daughter and bends so her face is right in line with Daphne's.

"Where. Did. You. Get. It?" Brenna's lips barely move, but the panic makes her voice sound like she's shouting the words.

"I don't know," Daphne mumbles again. Brenna whips herself upright and then lunges towards her daughter.

"We need to burn it," Brenna says. "Oh my God. I thought we were safe!"

"What? I don't understand. What do we need to burn? I have to go check on Mark, give him his medicine." I try to rush over and separate the two of them, but Brenna moves away first, clutching Daphne's toy as her daughter sits there looking terrified by how upset her mother is.

"The bear," Brenna shouts at me. "The bear from Darren's apartment!"

16

DAY 7
TOBIAS

I can't put it off any longer. With Darren gone, there's been this unspoken agreement between the adults at Granfield that I would manage the outdoor responsibilities as much as possible, and that Brenna and Margot would split what needed to be done inside with the children and for Mark.

We've been rationing our food, and although Brenna has asked me every night to come in for dinner, I still have enough to eat in my apartment. I'll have to get food from the manor house eventually though.

Until they run out too.

Which is why I need to do this before it's too late.

Brenna and I walked through the greenhouse on Day 3, after we'd finished disinfecting and the fire had burned low enough that we didn't have to worry about it spreading or sparking. We found nearly fifty different types of plants that Darren had sprouted from seeds or almost-full plants ready to go into the earth. Tomatoes and cucumbers, potatoes and butternut squash. Lettuces. Kale and spinach. Brenna had an app on her phone she'd downloaded that let her take a picture of the plant, and a few seconds later it spit out the name across the screen. It wasn't perfect—my mother grew sugar pumpkins every summer to make pumpkin pie at Thanksgiving, and I'm certain that whatever is growing vines across the furthest table of the greenhouse is not a pumpkin, even though that's what the app said—but it was better than trying to figure them out on our own, using the limited internet we have or trying to search out a gardening book in Darren's apartment. It was a small miracle that Brenna could get online as long as she did.

She explained it to me when I asked, something about towers and signal boosts and operating at peak capacity with entire cities on lockdown and everyone trying to work from home, but I still don't quite understand how any of that affects us way out here. All I know is that, since the lockdown order came, getting online has been sporadic at best and I'm really glad I don't have to try to run a company through a computer, like Brenna has to.

I was planning to plant the seedlings soon, now that the days are getting longer and the ground is thawing, but when I went to check on the plants two days ago there was something else in the greenhouse. Little white flecks of dust spread out on the green planters.

Aphids.

I know from my mother too that aphids are a death sentence for most plants. They'll eat the leaves, and then the stalks, and then the roots. Once seedlings are infected, there's nothing you can really do except give up on the plants—or poison the aphids.

But poisoning the aphids means that you have to poison the plants and the soil, which is obviously a tricky business.

When I told Brenna about all of this, she just stared at me with a look that made me want to melt into the floor and then asked me, quite nicely, if I could fix it.

So I'm fixing it.

In the gardening shed, there are lots of different chemicals. Lots of skulls and crossbones written across packages, promising to kill anyone who misuses them, which isn't exactly a confidence boost for me. But I have to do this. Otherwise we're going to starve.

Even though the internet's been spotty, late at night a few times I've gotten on—I figured Brenna wouldn't be trying to have meetings in the middle of the night, and I wouldn't be making it harder for her to work—and I've been able to see what's happening outside of Granfield.

People are sick. People are dying.

The National Guard is deployed through almost all major cities in the US. Grocery stores are ransacked and people are hoarding toilet paper.

There are a few headlines about families being attacked on roads, as they try to get to the border crossing and make it over into Canada. Some reporters are claiming that there are gangs forming, taking advantage of people sheltering at home and using this pandemic as an opportunity to take what they want.

A lot of gun stores have been emptied out.

The poison I need is in a bright blue bag, nestled on the bottom shelf next to the mothballs and the vermiculite. It says right on the bag that it's ideal for killing aphids.

I need to mix it with two parts water, and then spray everything down until its sopping wet. The aphids will die, but hopefully the plants will live.

A tight vice squeezes around the sides of my chest as I fill a spray can with the right proportions of chemical and water. When Darren came down sick, and we went through everything to clean away the potential infection he might have spread, I had to stop Brenna from soaking the seed starts and their containers in bleach. She'd been shaking, unwilling to listen to me and shouting that we needed to keep the children safe. That I was putting them in danger.

Margot eventually pulled her away, after Brenna started shoving and punching at me.

And now I'm poisoning the plants myself. The thought of just burning the plants and the greenhouse down flits across my mind. Fire is cleansing. We could start fresh.

That's something my mother said a lot after the trial.

"You need a fresh start," she'd tell me on the phone.

But I didn't want a fresh start. I wanted Colleen.

And we can't start fresh, unless we want to start ourselves straight into starvation.

I hoist the sprayer into the air, aimed at the tomato plants first. I swear I can hear the insects munching on the greens, on the food that we'll need. Their hungry mouths are making a symphony of destruction right here in front of me.

They need to be stopped.

I spray, and the mist flows over the plants and coats the leaves. I work meticulously, from table to table, until the entire garden of seedlings is treated.

Now all we have to do is wait.

I put the can back next to the shelves, but I don't empty it out. It says on the bag that multiple treatments might be needed, and that if I didn't see the white specks of the aphids reducing in number within twenty-four hours I'll have to hit them again.

Of course, the more times I spray them, the longer we'll have to wait before we can plant them, before we can hope to have any food to harvest from them.

I check to make sure the nozzle of the spray can is turned off, so it isn't releasing vapor into the enclosed space of the greenhouse, and then I head back to my horses.

It's time for their nightly feed, and my hands tingle at the thought of their rough manes slipping through my fingers, as though the world isn't crumbling around us.

I don't let myself think about what we'll do if the gardens die, and the only living things left at Granfield are the people. And the horses.

17

DAY 9
BRENNA

I've decided to have a dinner party.

The thought sounds ridiculous, I know, but the past week has been tough and I don't think my body can take any more unwelcome surprises. I desperately need something to look forward to, something I can control.

So I'm raiding our freezer and I'm going to make a pot roast, like my mother used to make every Sunday dinner back in Ohio, and then I'm going to pour a pitcher of iced lemonade and have all the people sheltering at Granfield gather around a table in the kitchen and share stories about their day and pretend that the world isn't just piles of ash and fire anymore.

I burned the teddy bear.

I still don't know how Daphne found it. She won't tell me if it's something Darren gave to her a while back, or if she found it somewhere.

All I do know is that we did not buy Daphne a teddy bear like that, ever—it's always been unicorns for her, since she was old enough to babble and point to what she wanted—and the bear looks terrifyingly similar to one that held a pride of place in Darren's apartment, like some remnant of a young field hand at Granfield manor from the last century.

I haven't been in to check and see if it's gone now, from his apartment. The teddy bear. I don't want to know, I suppose. And I am so tired of living in fear.

I need to get a grip on myself. I've felt like this for too long— well before we all became locked in at home, my husband and children and these two familiar strangers.

What should be three, a little voice in my head reminds me. *I did what needed to be done*, I tell that little voice. I pinch myself on the side until it hurts so much it burns and I'm certain to leave a bruise, but my head feels clearer afterwards.

Fear's been the constant filter I live my life through. Ever since the break-in that would have left Mark dead if Tobias hadn't happened to be out walking that night and seen what was happening through our front windows. It's this presence that sits far back enough that I can't see it clearly, but I can feel it there, like a figure stalking me on my way home in the dark, determining which turns I take in order to make it to the end.

If I can get a handle on everything, I can get us through this. I'm certain of it.

Which is why I'm down in the finished basement of the manor, peering through the secondary freezer for stew meat. I'm sure Greta bought some. There are flanks of veal, and lamb chops frozen into their crowned rings. Hot dogs for the children and chicken breasts individually packed, to cook and shred for my lunch salads.

The thought of fresh lettuce crunching under my teeth makes my mouth water. We finished the fresh vegetables and fruits three days ago, and have been relying on canned and frozen packages to supplement the rice and beans available in the pantry. I've never eaten so much starch.

Tobias said the treatment for the aphids seems to be

working, and that he'll be ready to plant the seedlings into the ground in another few days. I didn't ask him how long it'll take for everything to start fruiting, or for those round heads of green to be ready to pick. The weather has been warmer, and I've opened the windows throughout the house, including Mark's room, to air out the staleness of so many people being inside for so long. Still, it's definitely possible that we won't have enough to get us through until the garden takes off.

I wonder if anyone will bring that up at dinner tonight—the fact that I've made this sort-of fancy meal when we're getting closer and closer to running out of food?

The freezer door swings open too far as I try to push towards the back, hoping to find the stew meat somewhere on the shelves. I dressed up today in my normal work clothes, and the thin fabric of my silk shirt makes it feel like the cold air is rushing past my bare skin. I have a video meeting later today with my board—I told them I might have trouble connecting though—and I need to look like I'm not running scared from anything.

I don't usually wear foundation, but today I slathered it on in the hopes of covering the dark circles deepening each day underneath my eyes.

I finally give up on the stew meat and grab at a skirt steak instead. A flash of irritation flares up in me, because I don't usually have to make dinner. I'd work all day, rush home to see the kids and help them with their homework, and then scarf down a plate of whatever Greta had made before going over to Mark's rooms to see how he was doing. I was too busy to cook. I had a set limit to what I had to give to my life here at home.

And I work really well with limits.

"Mom?" The little voice is more a question than a request. Daphne's bright head pops from behind the doorway leading into the "rumpus" room where we keep an older set of couches and chairs from before the remodel, along with the extra freezer.

"I'm coming up in a minute," I call over to her, but I'm too late and she's already moved across the room and wrapped her arms around my legs.

"What are you doing?" she asks. She's shoved her mouth into the side of my thigh, and I can't help but notice the dark wet splotch forming on my pants.

I reach down and stroke her hair. "Looking for stuff for dinner. What are you up to?" I force brightness into my voice. Glancing at my watch I realize that I've spent too much time down here trying to play homemaker during the apocalypse and that my board meeting is coming up in just ten minutes.

"I was going to play Candyland. Want to play?" Daphne turns her face from my leg and up at me. She's always been an expert at pleading her case. "You said we'd play a game together if I worked on my lessons this morning."

I gently push at her shoulders, encouraging her to let go and allow me to move towards the stairs.

"I can play with you later, sweetheart, but right now I have to go put this in the fridge upstairs and then log on to my meeting."

Daphne lets go and trots alongside me. "Okay."

"Okay?" I say, not able to help myself. I wasn't expecting my daughter to give in.

"I'm going to go check on Margot," Daphne says. "Maybe she'll play with me."

We head up the stairs, and I let Daphne go first. The steak is forming a soft fuzz of ice crystals and my hand smarts a little from the coldness pressing into my palm.

"We're having pot roast for dinner," I tell her.

Her tiny body stops on the step above me and I have to grip the railing for a moment with my free hand to avoid bumping into my daughter.

"Can I have peanut butter and jelly instead?" Daphne asks as she keeps facing up towards the light of the open doorway.

"You can't have peanut butter, remember? Margot is allergic."

That was another mystery in this house of mine, although I'm fairly certain it was Felix who'd brought it home from school one day and hid it in the kitchen, too embarrassed to admit that some of his classmates had made it their business to try to get him in trouble.

We'd had a conversation with his teacher just before the pandemic hit. One of his classmates is deathly allergic to peanut butter, and all the families had received a note home at the beginning of the school year that we couldn't send food with tree nuts of any kind in our children's lunches.

I know Felix would have never done that on purpose. He would never hurt anyone.

But my son is also quick to point out how much smarter he is than other people, which is probably why the other kids at school dislike him, to the point of hiding a jar of peanut butter and package of Graham Crackers in his book bag and then telling the teacher about it in the hopes of getting him a week of detention, or worse—getting him suspended.

"Okay," Daphne says.

We're at the top of the stairs, and she turns left towards her room as I move right to the kitchen. I'll head upstairs to the library with my laptop for the meeting once I put the meat in the refrigerator to defrost.

"Okay?" I ask again.

"Bye, Mom," she calls over her shoulder, a skip in her step.

I turn towards the kitchen, disappointment in my daughter like a rotten fruit in my mouth.

18

MARGOT

The knife slices through the soft flesh of my thumb so swiftly that it takes a few moments before I realize I'm bleeding. It's not until I look down at the cutting board covered in a jumble of carrots and splotches of my own blood that I notice the pulsing throb in my left hand.

"Oh my God, you're bleeding!" Brenna rushes over to my side of the counter and, gripping my hand and holding it taut against the wood of the cutting board, she pulls me to the faucet and starts rinsing out my wound.

"I'm fine." I shush her away. "I'm a nurse, you know?" I crack a smile at her and press a nearby dish towel into my thumb to staunch the bleeding, but Brenna doesn't smile. She's pumping dish soap onto the board and carrots, and steam rises from the hot water pouring from the faucet. I reach over to dip my hand underneath the stream, and flinch back. Now my left hand is both scalded and sliced open.

I usually don't cook.

But Brenna was so excited when she came to find me in Mark's rooms and announce that she was making a special dinner tonight, and that everyone would sit down together at

7pm. Mark was having a difficult time talking today, but he didn't even need to ask if he was coming too. "We'll move you to the kitchen. A little special excursion, darling. It'll be good for you," she said to her husband, stroking his wrist over the fresh bandage I'd put on. His own wound was healing nicely, and soon there'd only be a thin white line where he'd managed to break open his skin.

"You should go wrap that up," Brenna tells me.

"It's fine." I flick my wrist, dish towel still cocooning my left hand. "I just need to hold some pressure on it until it stops bleeding."

"Be more careful next time." She stares into the mound of soap suds billowing from the sink. "We can't take risks like that."

There's a heavy pause between us.

I don't know where Darren's body is, or even if Tobias buried him. That evening, I'd checked on Mark and he'd asked me to close his windows because the air streaming in had smelled of smoke and burnt plastic.

"We're going to be okay." I say it for both our benefits. "We were protecting them."

Brenna reaches out and grips my hand, the one wrapped in the dish cloth, and squeezes hard. Very hard.

I think she's worried about me getting an infection or being more hurt than I'm letting on, so I move closer to her and put my forehead against hers. Our noses touch, and the soft breath from her mouth carries the fragrance of mint toothpaste and something wild and sweet, like the soft green stalks of dandelions my sisters and I would pull from the ground and suck on in the springtime.

"It's going to be okay," I repeat. I edge her hand away and pull the cloth from my own hand. The bleeding has stopped and all that's left of my error is a soft white slice of skin separated from the pad of my thumb. "Almost good as new."

But Brenna stays there, unmoving and unwilling to look at me. Which is when I realize that she didn't mean I needed to be more careful with myself.

"Until the gardens start producing, we have to account for every bit of food. We can't waste anything."

"I know. I'm sorry." I move back to the sink, taking a step sideways from her, and start to rinse the vegetables again. "I'll be more careful."

Brenna shifts the cutting board and the vegetables from my hand and walks back over to the central island counter in the kitchen. "You should probably go check on Mark, shouldn't you?"

Sometimes she talks to me as though I'm a complete stranger.

Sometimes it's like she can barely stand to look at me.

I think about two nights ago, tangled together in my bed. She came to find me that night. She'd wanted me.

But I correct myself. She'd wanted *someone*.

I set the knife down into the hot soapy water of the sink and slink off through the kitchen hallway. I'm not sure where I'm going, only that I need to get away from Brenna.

The carpet in the hallway glows with the light coming through the windows. I've spent most of the day in Mark's smaller rooms, talking with him about nothing in particular. I could tell that he was feeling lonely when he woke up this morning—Brenna had been in for a few minutes to announce her dinner plans, but she hadn't stayed for long because of a meeting she had with her company.

"I miss meetings," Mark had said, and I'd squeezed the soft ring of his ankle underneath the blankets as Brenna triggered the keypad and left.

I decide I could use some fresh air, and turn towards the outer door that leads from the main entranceway and the "grand" staircase. The chandelier hanging above the black and white parquet floor is enormous and imposing, and I'm thinking about how money seems to make things more beautiful than they deserve, when I bump into someone.

Such an enormous house, and I can't seem to find a quiet space to myself.

It's Felix, of course.

He's been pacing the rooms of the house these last few days. Sometimes I can hear him counting under his breath. Once I was sitting in the forgotten library, scanning the spines of the books hoping to find something to read that would let me escape from the thoughts that seem to clog my mind up at night when I'm trying to sleep, or waiting to see if Brenna will come visit me, and I heard him sweep by, murmuring "Six-hundred and forty-five" followed by a pause and a soft shuffle. "Six-hundred and forty-six."

Today I don't catch the number he's on. He may have been counting in his head, since I didn't hear him come up beside me. There are so many places in this house that seem to swallow the light. The more sunshine that pours through the windows, the deeper the shadows in the corners become.

And Felix seems to love lurking around in the shadows.

"I'm sorry," I say for the one-thousandth time today. Quarantine is making me way too pliant. "Did I mess up your counting?"

Felix eyes me like a rabbit caught in a snare. I smile and brush a lock of hair that's fallen in front of my eye, hoping to ease the nervous tension that surrounds him.

"You have blood on your face." He gives me a quick nod and then takes another step in the same direction he was heading.

There's a soft murmur in his wake, but again I don't catch the number he's on.

I pass a mirror in the hallway and dare to give myself a

glance. There's a wide streak of bright red smeared across my forehead and down towards my cheekbone. It must have come from my thumb when I brushed my hair out of my face.

I thought the bleeding had stopped.

When I look down there's another bead of blood sitting on my skin like a jewel. I go to suck it off with my mouth and hopefully stop the blood flow, but I'm too late and it falls like a single drop of rain onto the pristine white tile below my feet.

I don't bother to wipe it up.

Instead, I walk in the opposite direction of Felix and head through the front door, towards the open space of the fields.

19

TOBIAS

Julie's mane whips in the breeze flowing across the bright yellow field. The winter hay is turning green and peppered with bright yellow orbs as it overstays its place in the turned soil.

I'm hoping to figure out how to work the main tractor that Darren used with the harvest attachment, but it's harder to use than it seems. One look at the swinging blades underneath the housing told me I needed to be careful.

Colleen always thought that I was a little too impulsive. "Why don't you just stop for a moment and think it through," she'd tell me. The last time she said that she was rubbing at her stomach, our little glimmer stretching her skin, pulling out the fabric of her shirt like a promise you could hold in your hand.

I thought I listened to her when we were together—that I was a good husband—but memories do strange things the more you try to revisit them. They shift and stretch in ways you never expected.

Margot pats Jasmine's neck next to me. She's a vision of spring beside me, with her dark green sweater and sleek hair bouncing against her shoulders in time with Jasmine's stride.

The sun catches both of them in a pocket of light as the clouds move above us, and for a moment the two of them are the most beautiful thing I've seen in a long time. Even more beautiful than seeing those little white specks disintegrating on the plants in the greenhouse.

But not as beautiful as the way I remember my wife.

Not nearly.

Even still, I can't help but smile at the two of them, and Margot catches me looking over. She whips her head back to the front, focusing on where Jasmine's taking her, and I think I've ruined the moment. I want to call over to her that it's not what she thinks it is, but Margot shouts something over the snap of the wind that kicks up as we move further towards the edge of the woods.

"She's magnificent, isn't she?" she calls over.

She bends down again and gives another quick pat to Jasmine's broad neck, and I see the touch ripple through the horse's body out to the tip of her tail, where it shakes itself out in a whirligig of motion. Jasmine always has been a show-off.

We've been riding fairly slowly, strolling along the field, but at Margot's touch Jasmine seems to decide that it's time for her to show what she's capable of. Rearing back slightly, I watch the two of them canter down the field, headed straight for the tree line of pines that edges our open fields.

Julie whinnies underneath me, and I give her a tender squeeze with my heels.

"Okay, girl," I signal, and she doesn't wait a second longer. We're racing, and the cool air of the afternoon rushes through my body rather than over it. The speed acts like a release valve, and the tight coil inside my head unfurls the faster we go.

I cast another glance over to Margot, and see the same intensity on her face I've caught sometimes when I watch her sitting with Mark. She's determined to make this work.

I was in the stable when she came to get me, which was a surprise in and of itself. Before I got my sleepwalking under control there'd been a few awkward encounters in Margot's room—awkward and embarrassing and kind of awful really—so I'd tried to give her as much distance as possible afterwards. She'd apparently decided to do the same, because today was the first time she'd been in the stables since she'd arrived at Granfield.

I'd just been to check on the plants in the greenhouse, and was feeling a little giddy that the treatment was working. I'll be planting everything tomorrow, as long as the front holds off tonight. Brenna said we have enough food to last us until our crops start to yield something, but part of me thinks that she's spinning the situation.

She really wants me to come to this dinner party tonight. I hadn't planned to go though, because there's so much work to do out here and I don't really fit with everyone from the main house. Except for Mark, but he's not really going to be the belle of the ball tonight now, is he?

"Brenna cast me out of the kitchen," Margot explained as she walked up to the stables. "She apparently needs total control while she's cooking." Margot's face had been distant, a combination of disappointment and relief. "Could I go for a ride, do you think?"

She reached up to stroke Jasmine's nose. "I need to clear my head."

How could I say no to that?

So we suited up my two best girls and headed out. I wasn't about to let anyone near my horses alone.

Julie's breath comes harder as we canter along the edge of the field near the woods. There are lots of sticks down the closer we get to the tree line, and I call out to Margot to steer Jasmine further into the field. One misstep could catch a hoof or a leg, and horses don't come back from broken bones.

Margot hears me and nods, taking the reins in her hands and turning them away from the ancient pines and Douglas firs. A few maples are starting to bud, and the mixture makes the forest look like one of those paintings of dots that come together into an image the further you get from it.

Time to get back and admire the view from a distance, I think. I lean over and give an encouraging command in Julie's ear, promising her a few cubes of sugar—not too many, we're rationing, of course—when we get back.

As Margot makes the turn though, I watch Jasmine rear up on her hind legs. She's massive, like a thunderstorm bottled into the body of an animal. Every muscle flexes, and her silky fur shivers in waves of angry muscle.

Margot loses her grip and falls. When her body hits the ground it makes a thud so dull that it's like an insult to gravity. I try to stop myself, but all my mind can think of is dropping a sack of feed onto the floor—that bulbous round sound of something inanimate collapsing in on itself.

I halt Julie and immediately rush over to Margot. Both horses know the way home, and they pair up together quickly and start running away from the forest and back to the stable.

Margot's head is bloody, her arm bent in a strange angle behind her back. It might be broken, or she might have only fallen on it hard.

I call out her name. I bend down and listen for her breath.

She's breathing, she's in pain, but she can respond to what I'm saying.

She winces as she tries to gather a deeper breath.

I bend over to pick her up, thinking that I can carry her back to the stable—that I can't leave her here all alone. She says something, too raspy at first for me to understand it.

As I pick her up and find my way through the field as fast as I can without jostling her broken arm, Margot says it again, more clearly this time.

"Did you see him?" she asks. "In the forest. Did you see him watching us?"

20

MARK

The band of light arcs across the ceiling towards the right-hand corner of the room.

My hands and feet are locked in the straps sewn into the side of my bed. The restraints are there for my own protection, I've been told.

I remember that, at least.

I think I'm alone, but then someone emerges from the corner. It's hard to make out their face because they're backlit into darkness by the window behind them. I try to make a guess from the way they carry themselves, but I know it's futile.

My mind is becoming a rabbit warren of blank spaces.

Soon enough I'll be lucky to remember my own name.

I watch as they put on gloves. As they ready the needle and prepare the IV bag to give me whatever substance du jour they've decided on.

They tell me they're curing me, one dose at a time. I don't know if this is what they always tell me, or if this is a special revelation only meant for today.

There's no way to know if it's true.

My mind trips.

A stumble, a two-step shuffle, and then I'm gone, swallowed whole by the plans somebody has for me, into a deep and troubled sleep.

21

FELIX

"Why is he tied up?" My mother's strangled voice leaps out from the intercom speakers in my room. In all the rooms of the house.

"Margot, why is he tied up?" she shouts again. The air crackles with static and there's shuffling on the other end before the line goes blank. I move away from my telescope and move towards my doorway, but when I open it Daphne's there staring at me like a child in a Stephen King novel, blue dress and pinafore and perfectly tamed ringlets.

"Why's Mom yelling?" she asks.

"I don't know." I brush her aside and head towards Dad's end of the house. As I run through the hallway, down the main stairwell, and over the foyer into the separate wing with the keypad and blinking lights, I feel Daphne trail behind me. Not quite as fast, since her legs are shorter than mine, and also because she seems a little sulky. We haven't made up since our fight in the panic room. Not really, although I apologized and then Mom made me apologize again.

When we get to Dad's rooms, the doors are wide open and Mom's standing at the intercom, her white apron stained with streaks of red and brown and her hair tied into a wild bun on top of her head. I've never seen her like this. I didn't know she owned an apron.

Greta does, but hers are all colors and patterns. Mom's looks like something a surgeon would wear in the old Victorian shows Greta would watch sometimes on the TV in the kitchen while she made dinner.

Mom sees us and her face is like a shade coming down—or going up, depending on how you look at it. She shakes her head, smiles, and motions for us to come in.

"Everything's fine, sweethearts. I'm trying to find Margot. Have you seen her?"

I think back to what I saw through the telescope lens earlier today, before Mom did an all-points bulletin across the entire house. Part of me wants to tell her. Get it all out there. But another part knows it'd be better to keep it to myself. She already looks terrified.

I glance over at Daphne, who blinks her huge doe-eyes and tips her chin up towards Mom. "I think she went horseback riding with Tobias," she tells Mom. Blink, blink.

I stay quiet. I'm not certain of what I saw, anyway. And we're safe inside the house. That's why we have alarms and locks and keypads. I don't want to make Mom worry more than she already is.

Mom runs a hand through her hair, but she must have forgotten that she tied it up because her fingers catch on the elastic band. Most of her hair comes undone as she pulls her hand back down, and she snatches at the band to pull it out completely. It makes a ripping noise, and she winces as some strands stay stuck in the clasp of the elastic.

"I was just making dinner." Mom gestures to her apron with her other hand, shoving the hair tie into an unseen pocket in her pants.

"It smells delicious," Daphne says, and I want to punch her for it. There's nothing to smell but plastic packaging and expensive disinfectant. If I got close enough to Dad I could probably smell his cologne, which I think Mom or Margot sprays on him in the mornings, but I don't want to see Dad right now. The corner of his bed is visible from where we're standing in the outer room, but I don't hear any movement and he doesn't call out to us.

Mom follows my gaze.

"Your father's resting," she tells us. "I really need to find Margot."

There's a slam from somewhere in the house, and then two sets of steps rushing around.

Mom freezes, only for a split second. Then she whirls into action. She jumps in front of Daphne and me and propels the door closed with both hands. It's quiet for a moment, and I hear the soft hum of the locks engaging.

"Get inside with your father," she tells us, and Daphne and I obey.

"Is it happening again?" Daphne asks. "Are they coming for him?"

They are the whole reason we have all the security in the house, especially around where Dad is. Right when he first got sick, a group of people tried to break in and kidnap him. Mom's never really told me the specifics, and I somehow managed to sleep through the entire thing. The next day though, there were police cars and an ambulance with a big black bag covering a stretcher. I didn't realize it at the time, and Greta pulled me away from the window when she caught me staring out at what was happening, but of course it was a body underneath that cover.

When I looked everything up online afterwards, it turned out that I was only seeing the last of the dead men.

Mom's gone for what feels like an hour but I realize is

probably only twenty or thirty seconds—I read in one of my books that time is relative, and I feel like that's especially true when you think something terrible is happening. When she comes back she races past us and runs into the bathroom in the other room. I want to scream out to her, and ask her why she's leaving us again, but this time she's back in another second.

There's something dark and angled in her hand. It takes me a moment to realize what it is, and Daphne beats me to it.

"Mom, why do you have a gun?" She sounds more excited than frightened.

That's when the banging on the door starts.

Mom holds the gun between her hands, pointed at the door like someone in an action movie. She won't take her eyes off the door.

None of us can.

Except for Dad, I notice. He just stares blankly up at a streak of light on the ceiling.

22

MARGOT

I know what I saw.

That's what I tell Tobias through strangled gasps of air while he carries me to the main house. I know there's no other way for me to get back, but I can't help but flinch a little when he first goes to touch me. There are so many images swirling in my head, and one of them is Tobias staring with those dead, sleepwalker eyes at me from the corner of my room.

Nearby the two horses trot towards the stables. They went ahead of us at first, eager to get away from what we spotted in the woods, but now they seem to hang back. My horse keeps turning her head with her long neck, one round eye peering back until she finds Tobias and me hobbling along. Then she shifts to the front, and canters a few feet further into the meadow.

Tobias makes a whistling sound through his teeth, and both brown heads turn and their hooves stop. He repeats it, ending it louder and on an up-tone this time, and both horses pause for a heartbeat before they move together like one huge animal and trot to the barn. It takes them only a few seconds, it seems, before they're safely swallowed into their stables. I know I'm imagining it, but I swear I could hear the scrape and click of the stable door closing behind them, as though one of them was able to do it with their mind or had suddenly sprouted arms along with their improbably long legs.

Tobias grunts as he readjusts the weight of me across his shoulders. He's carrying me like a bride on her wedding day. My mother had a photo in her bedroom where my father held her the way Tobias is holding me. They were both smiling these wide grins, and the photo had little white speckles across it, which Teresa told me later were bits of confetti that people threw as Mom and my father left the church. I've seen a bunch of wedding photos since then—mostly on Facebook or Instagram, granted—and I've realized that it was strange for him to be carrying my mother out of the church. Most couples walk hand in hand.

It feels like a prediction, my mother needing to be carried into her marriage rather than walking out, equal and ready.

"We need to get you back to the house. You need to rest."

"I know what I saw," I tell Tobias again. I peer over his shoulder, the scruffy wool of his plaid shirt rubbing on the corner of my cheek. The forest looks abandoned. It's just nature, and wind, and tall grasses waving along.

There's no dark figure, reaching out from the edge.

But I wasn't the only one who saw it.

"The horses saw them," I add. I cough and a piercing flash of pain ripples around my chest. "I think a few of my ribs are broken."

Tobias stops. We're about fifty yards from the house. It's not a long distance, but it's long enough. His breaths come in deeper pulls, and beads of sweat have collected on his forehead. We've gone about a mile from where Jasmine threw me.

"Horses are easily frightened." He sets me down on my feet, looking into my eyes as a way of asking if I can handle standing for a few moments. I nod and he keeps a hold on my arm as I find my footing. Another sharp bolt of pain traces itself up the right side of my chest.

Probably three, maybe four ribs.

It's going to be hell to heal these up, I think. And then another thought flashes through my mind. Who will take care of Mark? Why was I so stupid, letting my cabin fever get the best of me?

I look up ahead at the house, its grey stone looming up like a monolith against the bright blue sky. Only a few clouds cover the wide expanse. If people weren't dying all over this country, it would be a beautiful day.

"So you think your horses got spooked by a shadow or something?" Tobias' grip tightens on me, and I fight the urge to squirm as I keep talking. "You think I'm seeing things?"

He pulls me closer to him, and for a brief moment it flashes through my mind that he's going to kiss me and that I'll have to fight him off with my broken ribs and my shaking, adrenaline-laced hands. But he doesn't kiss me.

Instead, he pulls me up into his arms, gentle as ever but still making me wince as my broken body realigns itself. "We need to get you back to the house."

"There's someone out there, Tobias." I don't know why, because we are in an open field and there's nobody around within hearing distance, but I whisper the words in his ear.

"The mind plays weird tricks sometimes," he responds, walking faster as we get closer to the house.

I have to say it. My heart drums, remembering the outline of the figure I saw in the woods. The heft to the shoulders. And the cough, mild, and rattled with the leaves in the breeze blowing through as Jasmine bucked me off.

"Are you sure..." I pause, and Tobias seems to ignore what I'm saying or be willing to let me fill the silence. His arms are warm against my back and legs, where he's supporting my weight as he takes me back to Granfield.

"Never can be sure of anything," he whispers back to me. The wind whips up again and snatches the last few syllables such that I have to assume what he said. He could have said "everything", or "anyone". I don't know.

I start again. We're almost to the back patio, and I hope the slashes of pain wracking my body will lessen once we're on more solid ground, and Tobias doesn't have to navigate the bumpy undergrowth of the field.

"Are you sure that Darren is gone?"

I can picture perfectly the dark imprint of the man in the woods. I'm certain it was a man. The figure was too big to be a woman. In the field, I swear I smelled a whiff of tobacco. The horses smelled it too, I think. Motor oil and freshly turned earth hung on the air.

My father smoked. That's what my sisters told me.

Darren did too, from what I can remember of seeing him out around the estate.

We've come to the patio, and Tobias almost hurls my body onto the ground, only at the last moment catching me up with his hands and lowering me with a bit more pressure.

He looks at me and his face is ashen, his mouth a grim divider. He looks certain of something, but his eyes are weak and liquid. It's like his body has mixed two pieces of his life, past and present on the same face.

"I'm sure," he says.

And he wrenches the door open and calls into the cool dark air of the house.

23

FELIX

"Where's Daphne," Mom screams. "Oh my God, where's my baby girl?"

Daphne's standing right behind Mom, but it's like she can't see her. Mom's eyes track across the room, staring blankly at the corners and walls. The gun in her hand glints under the special recessed lighting, and I see Daphne watching it with her eyes.

She doesn't move to knock Mom out of her trance, or whatever it is that's happening to our mother. My sister stands there, a look on her face that is pinched and, more than anything, mean. She looks kind of disgusted that our Mom is freaking out.

Not that anyone likes each other much at this point.

But we love each other. That's what family does. Dad reminded us of that all the time, before he got sick and had trouble focusing his thoughts. When you're family, you love each other. No matter what.

I have to remind myself of that sometimes, because it can be hard for me to feel things that other people feel. Like right now, Mom is screaming for Daphne and frightened about who is out there, and I seem to be relatively fine. Although, for some reason

I can't really tell you, I don't tell Mom that Daphne is right behind her. I keep letting her stare wildly out in front of her.

The voices come through the walls again, but they aren't loud, although there are rushing footsteps alongside them, which makes me think that either someone is running towards us but trying to sneak along at the same time—which is unlikely —or it isn't someone bad. Instead, it's something bad that's happened, to someone here at Granfield.

I do a quick assessment of my body, and my heart isn't racing and I'm not perspiring more than is normal for someone on the brink of puberty. There are no goosebumps on my skin, which is a sign of fear and our sympathetic nervous system shifting into fight or flight. I even have the time to think that goosebumps are called piloerections, and to consider how strange and kind of funny that is.

So it's all the more unexpected that, when I watch Mom's face shift from terror into understanding that it's only the nurse and the horse tamer outside, I manage to get distracted from keeping an eye on Mum. I'm not overwhelmed by anything. I don't have any excuse, except that I saw something move and I glanced away to try to catch it.

It was only Dad, shifting around in his bed and throwing his sheets out and over, like some sort of signal. Mom must have taken off the restraints for him before she called over the intercom. Dad doesn't look scared. He looks focused, like I do when I'm working a math problem and trying to find the solution that's written at the back of the textbook.

Mom says that the two of us look a lot alike, but I don't really see it. Not yet, at least. I keep hoping I'll grow into being like my father.

His mouth moves in the shape of words. Some days he can't talk as well as others. It's like something gets inside his body and shuts his voice and other parts of him down for a little while.

I go over to Dad for a small moment, listen to what he's trying to say and put my hand on his for a couple of seconds, like I've seen Mom and Margot do, and when I turn back to them, Mom and Daphne are in the other room with the outer door, and it's happened already.

The shouting from outside the door has stopped. Daphne must have come around, because Mom is holding on to her like she's never held anything more precious in her entire life.

Mom looks up and her eyes meet mine, and the relief I see in her face finally triggers something inside my chest. I run to her and let her pull me into a tense embrace. My mouth is pressed into Daphne's hair, which is kind of gross, but I don't complain. I just shut my mouth.

Mom's nails dig a little into my shoulder as she grips on to us, and then she lets go and walks over to the door. She swipes the key card. The soft thrush of the locks sifts through the air and she pulls the door open. Standing outside is Tobias, looking sweaty and upset, but otherwise fine. Next to him is Margot, leaning on his shoulder like someone's crumpled her up and tried to stretch her out again.

Daphne jumps in before anyone else can talk. "Why do you look so messy?" She eyes Margot.

"She had a fall out on one of the horses," Tobias tells my mom, ignoring Daphne.

I think about what my father whispered to me, a moment ago.

And it's not until then that I notice.

Mom's hands are free. She's not holding the gun anymore.

I scan the room, trying to track where she must have put it down when she reached out to hug Daphne, but I don't see it anywhere.

"I'll be fine," Margot says, but her voice is huskier than usual and there's a rasp to her breathing.

"She needs to rest." Tobias motions for me to come over and help him move Margot onto the couch where my mother sleeps sometimes.

My mother hasn't said a word. She blinks at Margot as she cringes and then spreads out on the couch.

"Where are the bandages?" Tobias asks, and Mom gives a small motion with her hand towards the entrance to the other room.

"I'll get them," Daphne offers, and runs over to my father's room. She's back a moment later with a huge roll of gauze, which means she must have remembered the drawer they're kept in in Dad's room. "Is this what you needed?"

Tobias takes the bandages, helps to unbutton Margot's shirt (I try not to look at anything besides her collarbone) and tells Margot to walk him through wrapping her broken ribs. That's why she's been having so much trouble breathing, I think.

It takes a few minutes, Tobias working quietly and my mother standing back, looking out into the middle distance, but eventually Margot's chest is wrapped and Tobias buttons her shirt back up.

A loud growl rumbles through the room. It's Daphne's stomach, and a hot flash of annoyance shoots through me. "When's dinner?" Daphne asks.

"Dinner's at seven," my mom says, her voice coming as though she's somewhere far in the distance, stirring a pot roast.

"There's something else," Tobias says. He's standing up now, so that Margot can have the entire couch to herself.

Margot turns her head slightly, and when her eyes meet my mother's I feel something electric flick through the room. My mother gives a shudder, like she's a computer screen waking from sleep. Finally, her eyes focus again.

"Something else?" she says.

I think of what my father said.

He has moments where he's paranoid. I know that. That's why I patted his hand.

"I saw someone, out in the woods," Margot tells us.

Daphne whines. "I'm so hungry."

I watch my mother reach behind her, and her fingers fumble at the waistband of her pants. The realization that washes over her as she grips for the gun and doesn't find it drains the blood from her face. She brings her hands up and links them in front of her, like she's saying a silent prayer. But she isn't.

"Where is it, Daphne?" she asks.

Daphne stares at her feet. "I said I wanted peanut butter."

There's that clench in my chest again.

They're coming. That's what my father mouthed to me. *They're coming.*

24

BRENNA

I am stirring a pot like some deranged housewife. I am actually wearing an apron, although it's utilitarian and all straight lines. I found it in the bottom of the drawer where Greta keeps her aprons, which were otherwise all sunshine and daisies with frills at the straps. I may not be sure of many things these days, but I can say with absolute certainty that I am not the kind of woman who wears frills on an apron.

Outside of that, who am I?

A woman who takes the gun her husband bought against her will and waves it around with her children in the same room.

A mother who raised a daughter mean enough to pretend to hide it because she didn't get what she wanted for lunch.

A wife who cheats on her husband.

An entrepreneur who ignores the urgent messages from her company and instead decides to make a happy family dinner out of stringy frozen beef and the last of the fresh vegetables for her two children, lover, invalid husband, and horse whisperer / replacement gardener.

I think I might be losing my mind.

"I'm hungry," Daphne says again.

"Dinner will be ready soon."

I've instructed her to sit at the kitchen counter and wait. She is in time-out, which I know is an effective parenting technique because I read about it in a parenting magazine once and I saw Greta use it with Felix to great effect. I'm not in the habit of disciplining my children in trendy fashion, granted, since I'm not home as often as I'd like—or I wasn't before all this. Hah, to be *not* home. Wouldn't that be a delicious gift, like someone making you a home-cooked dinner and then, after you've had your fill, saying there's not just one dessert, but two!

I'd kill for a slice of real chocolate cake.

I'd kill for a lot of things, truth be told.

A murderer. That's what I am.

And there's that flash of Darren's face. The one I see when I close my eyes at night. His pupils dilated, strings of hair plastered to his forehead. I see him when I wake in the morning too, but then his face is different. It's smooth and soft, and when I reach out to touch him and say that I'm sorry, all the flesh falls away and his skull stares back at me with two dark holes for his eyes. Scorch marks crawl up the sides of his skull like tattoos.

Nobody else is sick.

Of course it was worth it.

It turns out the gun had fallen underneath the couch and was covered by the little flap of fabric that brushes against the carpet. Tobias and I did a quick search and found it in a few minutes. I wouldn't let Felix or Daphne move, because I couldn't remember if I'd put the safety on it after we figured out who was shouting. I'd never actually held it, except for the one lesson Mark gave me when he first bought it.

He was still sore and bruised, but he'd insisted on standing behind me and helping me see how to place my hands around the handle and the pressure needed to pull the trigger fully.

We'd shot into a bale of hay that Darren set up for us near the machinery barn, far away from the house and the children and the stables. I remember Mark didn't want to scare the horses with the popping of the shots, which annoyed me at the time because the sound made me shake inside my chest even though I was the one making it. I wanted him to worry about me, which I suppose he was in a way.

The gun's in my locked bedside drawer now. I had to fight the urge to keep it tucked underneath my shirt in the waistband of my pants, with the smooth steel sitting against my spine like a talisman. You can't live in fear, I tell myself. As though telling myself this will change a lifelong habit.

"Why did you hide it?" I ask my daughter. I can't look at her, so I stare into the pot of gradually mushing potatoes and green beans and stringy meat. It looks disgusting.

Daphne presses her lips together. "I didn't hide it."

I hold my breath for a second. For two seconds. Pushing down the scream in my throat.

"Yes, you did. Margot and Tobias weren't in the room, and Felix was too far away from me to touch it. It had to be you."

I think back to that moment of pure panic, where I thought I wasn't ready as intruders came for my family again.

"Mommy, I swear I didn't do it."

She never calls me Mommy.

I feel myself soften. I have to remember how hard this is for everyone, but especially for the kids. How scary it must be, having a weapon waved around. Being stuck inside a house with this invisible microscopic enemy burning the outside world while inside there are people disappearing and a dying father and a mother who is doing things she's never done in front of them before.

I need to stay strong, I remind myself for the millionth time.

Felix looked petrified back in Mark's room. He's with Tobias, helping to get Margot settled back in her own bed in order to rest, but before he set off with them down to the other end of the house, I tried to catch his eye and give him something of a reassuring look. Not a smile, but a quick nod that would help him believe that everything is okay. But as I tried to set my face into something resembling calm, I saw his eyes staring back at me as though I weren't even there. It was like he was watching something unfold inside his head. Something nobody else could see.

Maybe I'm assuming Daphne was trying to cause trouble. It wouldn't be the first time I'd projected some sort of grown-up intention onto her. The counselor we worked with to help with Daphne's tantrums said as much. Part of Daphne's issue was my issue, thinking that things she said or did, like ignoring me when I told her it was bedtime or forgetting to pick up her dirty pajamas from the floor, were personal attacks against me. "She's just a child", the counselor would say, and I'd bite my tongue.

"I understand if you were scared of it," I tell Daphne now.

She bristles at this, as I should have known she would.

The mixture in the pot has come to a boil and I turn down the heat to let it simmer. No one will want to eat this.

I've wasted all the ingredients.

"I wasn't scared." Her bottom lip sticks out in a way that would be adorable. She looks so much like me when I was little. And yet, there are parts of her that seem to have grown from some other place, outside of Mark and me. I don't believe in magic or changelings, of course, but there are days where I wonder if I really know who my daughter is.

She tips her head down and mumbles something into the table.

"What did you say?" I'm trying to be patient. I'm thinking this is her way of confessing. Even still, as I wait for her to repeat what she said, I try to picture my lovely sensitive daughter reaching out impulsively and grabbing the metal handle of the gun, and thinking quickly enough to shove it under the couch.

It's not hard to do, but maybe that says more about me than her.

My daughter looks up from the table. "Mom, I think it was Darren."

"What?" A burning smell fills my nose. I bend over as I gag from the stench of fire scorching muscle and bone.

"It's burning," Daphne says calmly.

I heave in a clean breath of air. The stove is off. Nothing is burning.

"Dinner time," I call out into the silent house, because what else can I do?

25

MARK

W hatever they've given to me has worn off a little. My mind feels crisper, like a shard of glass in the sun.

Everything around me is enhanced and sharpened.

There are voices downstairs. They've decided to leave me up here, but not after a heartfelt visit from every able member of this house. The children, and Tobias, and my doting wife.

The friendly nurse who holds my hand sometimes wasn't there though. Margot.

I was guilty of it too, you know. Back when I was around other people. Assuming that someone who wasn't able to talk much, or correctly, was somehow also hard of hearing. I remember there was a secretary who worked for an exec friend of mine—some guy whose name I can't even remember now—and she had a terrible stutter. I'd waltz into the entranceway from the elevator and she'd manage to eke out a "Hello, Mm... Mm...Mister S...S...Stone." And then she'd smile.

I would then, without hesitation, shout back to her as if she were standing across a busy street, "Good morning, Nancy!" It was so loud that she'd noticeably flinch. One time, I was apparently so exuberant that a blush rose all the way up her neck and into her cheeks while she opened the door and silently gestured with a hand that I could go in. At this point the redness had spread up her neck and into her cheeks, and I remember thinking that it must have been hell for her growing up. Children can be monsters.

Serves me right, now that my thoughts keep getting caught inside my mind, that even my own wife talks to me as if I have the vocabulary of a two-year-old paired with the hearing of a retired rock star.

"Darling, we can't move you into the kitchen." She'd said this as though I were being told I was dying, which apparently I am too, but that doesn't matter right now. Slow, halting, and loud. Brenna has the most beautiful eyes—blue with a ring of green like a hidden jewel at the center of the iris. I've stared into those eyes more times than I can remember, naked and calm after our lovemaking, clinking champagne to celebrate another merger of our brilliant minds, locking onto each other after Felix, and then Daphne, were born.

But now, all I see when I look at my wife is disappointment.

And pain.

"Sorry you can't make it to dinner." Tobias emphasized each word with a nod. "I'll bring some up for you later."

Brenna put her arm in front of Tobias—all four of them were circled around my bed, Brenna and Tobias on one side, Felix and Daphne on the other. "I'll take care of it."

If looks could kill, then Tobias would have been flailing on the floor.

I'll admit. I play along sometimes with it.

I barely said a word while they were there, and I pretended to stare off into the distance for most of their visit. It's easier than fighting the muscles in my body that are trying to convince everyone around me that I'm an invalid, and that my mind and body are both metaphorically crawling off somewhere into that good night.

Plus, people pay attention less to me then.

Only Felix looked at me differently. I'm sure he was thinking about what I'd told him earlier, when Brenna thought we were under attack and she got the gun from the safe. I watched everything unfold with a certain bit of triumph surging through my body, because she'd fought me hard on getting that gun. Even after we'd been invaded, and I'd ended up in the hospital for a longer stay than usual. Even after the security system and keypads, the bars on some of the ground floor windows and the flood lights that can be set to be motion triggered, she still didn't want to have a gun in the house.

"It's a weapon, Mark," she kept telling me, as though that were a valid argument.

And I'd told her that was exactly the point.

But I can't keep waiting here, taking it literally lying down as my body eats away at itself. Death is coming for me. It's coming for all of us, if I don't do something about it. Caring for others has never come naturally for Brenna. My family needs me.

That's why I called over to Felix, while Brenna was distracted by thinking some outsider was getting in and about to kidnap her ailing husband. Again.

I knew it was only Tobias and Margot. That's the other irony of my situation. Everyone treats you like you're going deaf—in fact, like all your senses are degrading at once—but lying here in this bed, without a view of anything really but the ceiling of this well-appointed room, has honed my ability to hear to a fine edge. I can hear glasses clink in the kitchen, and know that it's Felix pouring himself the last of the milk.

I can hear Margot, walking outside my children's bedroom doors at night.

I can hear my wife, moving towards a bedroom that isn't her own.

And I can totally fucking tell when the voices streaming up the stairs and into my suite of medicalized, double-security lockdown rooms are only Tobias and the nurse.

I told Felix that someone was coming because he's a smart kid, and if he thinks that our family is in danger, then he will figure out a way to fix it. I went to all his science fairs and signed the checks on the science tutors. Brenna and I bought him that telescope together, and before I was chained to this bed I'd catch him staring out, not at the sky but at the ground, watching the people who kept Granfield running.

Learning how people work.

You see, I told him people are coming because he needs to be scared, because somebody in this house is trying to kill me.

26

DAY 11

TOBIAS

I couldn't sleep last night. I just lay there, tossing and turning around in my sheets until they were hot and damp. I must have eventually slept at some point, but today I'm achy and it's like someone has stuffed cotton inside my head. I put deadbolts on my doors after the sleepwalking problems last summer, so at least I know I wasn't out wandering—it always got worse when I was sleeping less.

None of that matters though, because there's no stopping the day ahead coming, which is both a comfort and a curse. Colleen used to have trouble sleeping too, and we'd lay there awake together in bed, staring into the blackness and holding hands. It was kind of romantic, and while life pulled us in different directions it was a comfort to feel her hand in mine during those long nights.

Once she was pregnant though, she slept like a baby, which left me alone when I couldn't sleep. That made it harder.

I get up and pull on a fresh shirt and the same jeans I wore yesterday. There haven't been any issues with our running water, and Greta apparently bought laundry detergent in bulk so we're fine there, but I've noticed Margot and the children recycling their outfits day to day, and my jeans aren't dirty.

There's a fine mist covering the fields when I glance out the window, and so I tug on a sweater over my T-shirt before I head out the door. It's not far to the stable, but I know something is wrong before I'm even two steps out my door, because the stable door is open.

I always close it at night. I don't want foxes or other unwelcome guests wandering in and hurting my horses. Their horses, I suppose—Mark and Brenna's.

But, *my* horses, all the same. They're tough but fragile creatures, and in the stable they're exposed more than people realize. Fenced in but also kept from getting out.

My boots make a strange click clack on the gravel as I run over, and although I know that it's probably because I haven't slept well last night, or for the last several nights—not since, well... I stop myself from thinking again of Darren. I can't change what's happened.

The past is the past. People get hurt. People die. People do things they never thought they'd be capable of.

There's a strange smell when I arrive inside the stables. I do a quick scan and all the horses are accounted for. Jasmine and Julie are snug in their pens, and the dark heads of their friends are lined up on either side down the length of the stable.

But that smell. There's a tang in the air, like metal that's been buried deep in the ground and unearthed.

I look again at Jasmine, and that's when I notice that even though her head is bent and she isn't nervously pawing at the ground, there's something wrong and she knows it. Her nostrils flare, and as I move closer to her she lets out a sound like nothing I've heard before.

Another terrible memory flashes up, of the afternoon I came home to surprise Colleen and take her out to lunch, only to hear her crying out from our bedroom. I thought she'd gone into some sort of false labor or that there was something wrong with the baby. I rushed down the hallway and through the closed door, and found her and our next-door neighbor, Jack Minnigan, thrashing and writhing on our bed, so distracted by what they were doing with each other that they didn't even hear me come in.

I could have shouted out, and gone and hauled that man off of my visibly pregnant wife and told them both that I'd seen everything—obviously—and to get the hell out of my house. But I didn't. Instead, I slinked out the door, closed it quietly behind me, and went back to work. When I came home that night, Colleen had made homemade spaghetti and meatballs for dinner. She kissed me deep on the mouth as I stepped through the door, and before we could eat dinner I had her in the bedroom again, trying to erase the traces of him from her body.

I know it's terrible, and wrong, but that's what I think of as Jasmine cries out into the soft air of the stable, where blood has mixed with fresh hay and the sweet bite of horse manure: me trying to take possession of my wife again.

I check Jasmine first, and then Julie. Neither of them appear to be hurt. It's not until I head further down the aisle between the stalls that I realize what's happened.

The body was hidden behind a rack of saddles and I don't see it until I move deeper into the stable. Bile rises in my mouth as I take in the two eyes staring back at me, clouded with death, one slightly bulging out as though there was some great pressure behind it, but the rest of the face perfectly serene and unharmed.

I reach out to touch the bright fur, and it's coarser under my fingers than I thought it would be. Blood has pooled all around the fox's body. It's hard to tell exactly what happened in the dim light slipping through the windows, but it appears that someone slit its throat and let its life pour out onto the floor of the stable.

I wonder if it was the same fox I'd seen wandering the fields around Granfield. The one I made sure to close the stable doors to at night, so that the harm it caused would stay outside the walls.

I wonder how someone could have caught such a fiercely defensive creature.

There's a noise that comes further down, where the last of the pens are. A sort of tinkling rustle, and again all I can think of is how Colleen made an extra plate of spaghetti that night to take over to Jack, "Because he's all on his own." I was the one who pulled the tin foil from the drawer and stretched out the piece to wrap around the plate. Thin metal, crinkling along the edges of food that was never meant for me.

I grab a shovel in my hand and move as silently as I can towards where the sound is coming from. Jasmine rustles in her stall. When I get to the end of the stables though, there's no one there.

But the back door where we slide bales of hay through is open, the tack for some long-forgotten horse swinging off of its peg even though there's no whisper of wind.

I move the fox's body out of the stable and bury it in the earth a few yards from the greenhouse and the garden plots. It'll feed us one day.

27

DAY 14
BRENNA

I can't hear anything. His voice comes like it's traveling through thick cement walls. Like we're prisoners in adjoining cells.

I shake my head and the world snaps back into place.

"Someone killed a fox." Tobias' voice comes through clearly this time. He's staring at me with that way he has, where his eyes seem to look at only one side of my face. I never noticed it before, but now it's all I seem to see when we talk. Which still isn't as often as you'd think, given that we're trapped in this house and grounds for the foreseeable future.

"What?" I feel like one of the children being told they'll have to eat lentils for breakfast now we're out of cereal and store-bought bread. I'm all petulance and disbelief.

"It was a few days ago."

He breaks his gaze from mine and stares out into the middle distance. We're standing outside the greenhouses. Inside, many of the plants are ready to go into the ground, we think. Tobias has already planted some of them in the plowed plot over the last few days.

"Why didn't you tell me?"

I want to shove him hard, with both my hands pressed firmly against his broad shoulders. I want to slap his face, because he's the only person in this house I could get away with pushing around. I've discovered that Tobias doesn't care if I'm nasty to him. He doesn't have to love me, like the others are supposed to. We just have to tolerate each other in order to feed our group. It's a relief, in a way, to have someone I don't need to pretend to be perfect for.

I think of Margot, still bedridden while her ribs heal. I've been avoiding her as much as I can. Bed rest does not agree with her. And also what she supposedly saw out in the field when the horse bucked her off—I don't want to talk about it or what it might mean. The night it happened, the night I made that sour sludge of a stew, and Daphne insisted that it was Darren Margot saw in the woods as a way of distracting me from the task at hand, which was figuring out whether Daphne had touched the gun, I decided to confront Tobias out in the stables once the children were in bed. He assured me that there was no way Darren was out there in the woods. "It was just shadows," he'd told me. "Or maybe a snake along the edge of the field. Horses spook easily." But now everything he said seems to be in question.

"I didn't think it was that important. You've had full nursing duties pretty much, and I've been trying to get the garden growing. I didn't want to scare you unnecessarily."

"You said some*one*, not something."

I think about how exposed I felt the night of Margot's accident, wielding that gun like a maniac while I thought someone was rushing up the stairs to come and drag us away. I think about men in black masks, speaking to each other in some language I've never heard before, holding a gun to Mark's head.

Tobias shrugs, but I can tell he's pretending that it isn't a big deal. He tells me about finding it in the stable, about smelling the blood on the air and thinking at first it was one of the horses that'd been hurt. "Its throat was slit. There's no way an animal could have done that. It had to have been a person."

I blink twice, because all I see is blackness for one heartbeat. Two. Three.

Tobias doesn't say anything. And then colors come back and the rich brown of the upturned soil and the ridged gray of the outbuildings behind sharpen into focus.

"And you didn't think to tell me until now? There's somebody roaming around, waiting for us. Margot saw them in the woods, and you convinced me it was nothing. And now there are animals being slaughtered! Whoever this is, they're taunting us, like it's some sort of sick game."

I really do shove him this time. Hard. He stumbles back, his boots catching on a rock strewn in the lawn around the greenhouse, and then he falls. He catches himself with his hands, but he must have hit himself in the stomach when he landed and knocked the air out of his lungs, because he lays there for a moment. I look around, and the edges of the rocks poking up from the grass twinkle with small crystals in the sunlight. They're just within reach. I could bend down and grab one, feel the smoothness in my hand. It wouldn't take much to do it.

I squeeze both my hands into tight fists.

"I'm sorry," I tell him without making eye contact. I stare at a cloud passing overhead, fat and cottony against the blue sky.

"I know you have children." Tobias stands up and brushes a few blades of grass off his shirt and jeans before continuing, like he's figuring out what to say next. "That's why I didn't tell you, at first. But something else has happened now, and I think you need to know about it."

"You mean something besides my family being stalked in our own home."

I pace back and forth, wearing a groove into the grass with my steps. My fingernails are bit to the quick, but I keep finding myself biting at them anyway. There's a riot inside my body that's been building and building and now it's gotten so loud that I have to strain to hear my own voice inside my head.

You're losing control. The thought breaks through the surface, followed quickly by another one: *You're failing them.*

"I don't think anyone is stalking us." Tobias looks at me as he says it. Right at me, without that strange shift of his gaze, and I shrink back involuntarily, like I'm worried he can magically read my thoughts.

"Come with me." He gestures with his hand, and moves across the path by the greenhouse and into the copse of trees that separates it from the main house and other barns. "I think you need to see it first."

I follow him along the path. It's only a short distance, but still I find myself having trouble keeping up with his long strides.

Inside the grouping of trees it's darker than out in the open. The sun barely peeks through the tips of the treetops. Tobias moves off the path, into the soft grass that grows under the pines. It's longer than out in the rest of the lawn, and dew collects on the tops of my shoes as I step through it.

And then there it is, nestled in under one of the largest pines, almost entirely hidden by the skirt of the tree's branches.

Tobias turns towards me. "This wasn't here when Margot and I went for that ride. I know because I spent part of that morning stripping out the dead branches from these trees."

I see the fresh cuts along the trunk of the tree, above the arranged objects he's brought me to see. The cuts are still pale against the dark of the tree's bark. A small part of my mind scratches at something normal and positive to say.

"You did a nice job clearing the dead away."

Tobias flinches. He knows I'm deflecting. Because, if what we're looking at wasn't here before Margot fell off the horse and became bedridden, and there's no boogeyman out in the woods, then that only leaves me, Tobias, and the children as capable of making this thing.

I bend down, my legs shaking, and force myself to take a closer look. There's a doll-size table that I recognize from the children's playroom. It goes with a set of chairs, and Felix and Mark used to play tea with his stuffed animals when he was little.

On top of the doll table is a doll with long brown hair dressed in a Victorian-style corset and skirt. It's one of those American Girl dolls that Daphne was really into playing with last summer, but has since been left sitting in a pile at the back of her closet.

Your children are spoiled, a voice whispers around me and I beat it back.

The doll's eyes are crossed out with two large, black X-es. Her white dress is smeared with brown streaks, which I don't need Tobias to tell me are probably blood. There are a few kitchen candles melted into the top of the table.

A small paring knife lies next to the doll. As I look closer, I see small slits cut into the plastic running along both of the doll's legs.

Tobias leans over me, blocking the bit of light in this close terrible space.

"It looks a lot like Margot, doesn't it?" he says.

28

MARGOT

"What do you mean you found an effigy of me?"

I'm trying to stay calm, but ever since my fall and then needing to stay in bed inside this oppressive mansion, tension has run constant laps up and down my spine.

"Tobias found it. I'm sorry, but I thought you should know." Brenna's mouth sets in a mean line. You'd never know that my lips had touched hers from the way she's talking to me. No one would be able to see that we'd held each other close, naked and breathless in the night, more times than I can even remember at this point. Although not recently. Not since this all happened, except for that one time.

I'm not sure if she's telling the truth.

"I need to see it." And suddenly that energy replaces everything else moving through my body. This need to picture what the hell someone has constructed out there in order to hurt me, or—is this even possible?—worship me. Or both, I realize.

My head spins a bit and the deep ache in my chest rises as I force as deep a breath as I can manage.

You are strong. You are capable. You are healing.

My sisters and I would chant the first two to each other, whisper it in each other's ears at bedtime as we kissed each other goodnight and the older ones tucked the younger ones in, including me, while our mother sat alone in her darkened bedroom and coped by pretending her family didn't exist. The third I've added these last several days.

They say nurses don't know how to care for themselves, but I've never been typical about anything. After watching my mother for so many years, I know how to take care of myself in order to take care of others.

I wish I could call Teresa right now. Hear my oldest sister's voice. She always knew how to set me going in the right direction. She always knew what to say.

Unlike my mother, who never said anything.

"You can't move. You need to rest." Brenna sits down on the foot of my bed, and for a moment I think we're going to have a flash of tenderness in the midst of this horror. I know she's married, and that she loves her husband, but I also think there's room inside for me.

But it's not that. I've misread the situation, again, with my wishful thinking.

Her eyes won't look at me—they keep flitting around the room, landing on the top of a dresser or the corner of the bedpost. Not on me. She shifts further on the edge of the bed so that no part of us, even through the downy comforter, is touching.

She has more to tell me.

"I think we should move you into the secure wing, with Mark."

A brief wave of relief washes over me, because I thought it was going to be some other gruesome addition. I don't mind being closer to Mark.

"All right. But I still would like to see what this thing is."

"I didn't take a picture of it." Brenna stands.

"Could you take one? I'd really like to see what's happening out there." I gesture towards the window, and then wince at the pinching in my torso.

You are strong. You are capable. You are healing.

I want to go back to normal. Sitting in this bed all day, with only my thoughts to keep me company, is killing me.

"I don't think that'd be a good idea."

"Why?"

"It's too awful."

She gives her head a slight shake, and her blond hair falls in shiny waves over her shoulders. I'd been so preoccupied that I hadn't noticed Brenna's appearance. She looks better today than she has since we went into lockdown. She's dressed in one of her going-to-work outfits, and her skin has a creamy pink glow.

Her eyes though. Her eyes are dull and distracted, still flitting all over the room and avoiding me.

I wonder if there are worries—terrors—regrets—humming through her body like they are mine. I wish she'd talk to me about them. I suddenly want to scream, "I'm here for you!" but I control myself. That's another important lesson I learned growing up: you can't force someone to love you.

I try to sit up in bed a little. It feels unmatched to be lying down while Brenna looms over me, dictating these important details of my life. Controlling what I can and cannot know. I push away the nasty thought that suddenly rises to the surface —that she came here to frighten me on purpose.

"So why tell me about it at all? I don't understand."

She breathes in deep through her nose, like she's dealing with one of her children throwing a fit. My hands clench into tightly balled fists. The pain in my chest throbs away.

"I needed to give you an explanation of why we're moving

you to be with Mark. Why it's better for you to be behind the secured doors."

"And you couldn't think of any other reason to explain why you're moving me?" I counter.

Brenna gives an exasperated sigh. "I don't need to listen to this," she says as she turns for the door. "We'll get you moved sometime this afternoon."

"Wait," I call out. Brenna pauses, her back still turned to me. A hot flush of embarrassment rises at how desperate I sound. "What's happening to us?"

I'm more than aware of the pleading in my voice, but I can't control myself. This situation—the lockdown, the isolation, being injured and bedridden—I'm more vulnerable than I've ever been. It's ironic, considering the reason I answered Brenna's ad and actually came here to Granfield. Life can change so much in nine months.

"What do you mean?"

Shards of ice run through her voice.

I swallow, hard. *Do it*, a voice tells me. *Get it over with.*

"You and me." I try to smile, but the muscles of my face won't work properly and my mouth twists into something else. Something between a sneer and a sob. My vision blurs as I push back tears, and I want to slap myself. "What's happening to us?"

I choke out the last word.

Brenna's face is a mask. Unreadable. She's crossed her arms over her chest and her body stands tall and dark as she leans against the door, framed by the light from the hall.

I wait for it, and then it comes. Just like I knew it would.

"There is no *us*," Brenna tells me.

I wait until the door closes, and her footsteps pad down the hallway away from me, before I let the tears out, silently sobbing into my pillow like a child for longer than I'd like to admit.

The rage comes later, like I knew it would.

29

DAY 15

FELIX

I know I shouldn't be doing this.

I know that it's wrong.

But someone needs to do it, and Mom is too freaked out by something she and Tobias found in the woods and Margot's stuck in her room. I have no idea where Daphne is, which is probably best.

I checked things out from my telescope first. Tobias is in the greenhouse, doing something with the plants. He's been spending more and more time there, which I figure is probably a good thing, seeing as we're going to rely on the gardens for food.

I got online last night for a few minutes before Mom came on the intercom and told me to get off. I don't know how she knew I was on, but she did. She's been having more and more meetings, sometimes for hours. She goes into that small library that nobody used to use, locks the door (I know because I tried to come in one time), and stays there talking to her screen. I only catch phrases when I press my ear to the door. It's easier to listen in, now that Margot is laid up with her broken ribs and Daphne is off playing with her imaginary friends. The walls of our house are thinner than you'd think, given that it's a "historical" home. Early in the morning I'll hear Daphne's angel-voice cutting through the air into my brain.

"Now, what did I tell you?" she'll say. "That's not how we do things here. Take a sip of tea. Eat your sandwich—it's peanut butter and jelly...I don't care if you don't like it. Now close your eyes, it's bedtime." And so on and so forth.

The only imaginary friends I had were kids at school who I thought liked me, but who ended up being liars. It was a whole other kind of pretend.

I walk down the hallway, past the little library where the door is closed and Mom is talking to someone. I have a key card for Dad's rooms—I borrowed it off the nurse we had before Margot, but then Mom realized the nurse didn't have her key card and fired her for a breach of security or something like that. I'd felt terrible, but I also didn't want to be locked out of rooms in my own house. Plus I got to visit Dad whenever I wanted to once I had the key card. I'm very careful about when I go in, so Mom hasn't figured out yet that I have a copy. Dad won't tell her. He likes when I visit, or at least it seems that he does.

But I'm not heading to visit Dad. I need to go and check out Darren's apartment.

I went into the medical wing late last night and got a gown and a mask and some gloves. Besides, when I checked the Centers for Disease Control website last night for those few minutes I got online it said that the virus can't live on surfaces for longer than twenty-four hours.

Anything in that apartment that was contagious should be long dead by now.

The house feels abandoned with Margot laid up and Mom hiding away. I walk softly in my socked feet, but there doesn't seem to be much of a point to keeping quiet, because there's no one around to hear me. That's something no one tells you about the end of the world—how lonely it can be, even if you're with your family.

I count the steps as I go. It's something I've started doing, to keep track or maybe just be in control of something. The same science book where I finally forced myself to read virus vectors and the CDC's "ground-breaking virology research" had a section on the biology of psychiatric illnesses. There was one part that talked about motivation and obsession, and it said that human beings crave control more than anything, and that when we are in situations out of our control we'll create opportunities to exert influence and power, even in small ways.

It makes sense to me. I always feel calmer after I count my steps. And going from one end of the house to the other makes it seem like I am king of the castle or something like that.

There's no place I can't go.

I wonder whatever happened to that nanny who left all her books here in that attic room. Maybe she's saving lives.

Maybe she's already dead.

I walk out the front door, passing the two huge urns on either side that used to have massive bouquets of fresh flowers. Now they're full of drooping husks of whatever was in them before the floral deliveries shut down. Even dead, the flowers are taller than me. Although I've been hungrier and hungrier these past few weeks, which usually means that I'm growing, it could also mean that we don't have as much to eat in general.

It seems strange, that my body could be getting bigger and stronger while everything around me is falling apart.

It feels like spring and the air smells sweet from all the trees and bushes blooming. Everything seems so happy outside that I have to fight the urge to run to the building where Darren's apartment sits on top. Gravel is so noisy when you rush across it, and I don't want Daphne catching on to what I'm doing and insisting she come with me.

She's *kind of the worst.* That's what the kids at school would say.

Some days I don't like having her as my sister. That's what I would say.

The pocketknife in my jeans tugs at the fabric as I move across the grounds. Dad gave it to me for my birthday last year, and I like to run my thumb against the smooth metal, back and forth like a pendulum. Or a worry stone. I keep walking like I'm some kid enjoying the sunshine.

The apartment doorframe is in shadows when I get there, which is lucky for me because no one can see me pick the lock with my knife. I didn't know how to do that before this quarantine, but I've been learning how to do lots of things since we've been stuck here together. You'd think, after Dad ended up in the hospital and Mom brought in all the special security barriers, that I'd have started carrying the knife with me then. Maybe I should have, but I didn't.

It's strange how some things scare you and other things roll off you like they were a dream that disappeared when you woke up.

It's really easy for me to open the door. The lock is a twisting doorknob lock, which I could probably have picked with one of Mom's bobby pins, to be honest. There's a sign taped to the door in handwriting I don't recognize.

"Stay Out" is written in block letters.

It's like my mom doesn't understand us at all.

Of course one of us is going to go in if she tells us not to. Disruption is in our blood. That's why our family is so rich. Both Mom and Dad weren't afraid to go against what other people were saying about their businesses. They'd talk about it at dinner some nights, when we still had family dinners. It's funny how grown-ups will forget that their children are listening, even when you're right there sitting next to them. I heard all about the lawsuits and the investment risks and some watchdog group saying Dad's company wasn't following labor codes overseas. And then I heard about how they'd won, and how much richer we were going to be.

When I open the door the air in the apartment hits me immediately. Musty and stale. I pull the mask and gown and gloves from underneath my sweatshirt, keeping them close to my chest, and step inside.

30

MARK

The day they came for me was the first day that felt like spring. It was the day after Daphne's sixth birthday. We'd given her a new tea set and a huge stuffed unicorn. That night I read her bedtime story, *The Twelve Dancing Princesses*, where the princesses disappear at night and fool all the princes who try to catch them.

I was laid up in bed with what I thought was just fatigue or a cold or something like that. It'd started coming on after dinner that evening, and I'd pushed through it until I almost collapsed into bed. I'd assumed it would pass, like all the other times I'd been sick.

I was wrong.

Brenna and I still shared a bedroom, and a bed, although she was already up and somewhere else in the house. I was on my side, huddled under the covers and wishing the pain in my head to go away and for my legs to move. That's when I felt the hand cover my mouth and the hard coolness of the gun's barrel pressed into my temple.

"Come with us, and nobody gets hurt," a disembodied voice said. I still had the covers over my eyes. I couldn't see who was grabbing at me, and so my instinct was to push out against them, which was a mistake.

I didn't have the energy to fight this person. I was sick, and getting sicker, although I had no clue my body was going to keep on betraying me, like some unfaithful lover.

Doctors still can't quite pinpoint it down. I've heard MS, Huntington's, general neurodegenerative disorder. Really, though, none of these damn labels matter. I'm dying. Full stop. I can't enjoy anything that I once loved.

Not my work, or my children. Not my wife.

But these people didn't know that at the time. Most people still don't know it.

And so they came to take me, hold me for ransom, and get their due.

They were trained fighters or some other type of mercenary. Afterwards we were told that they were Chechnyan or Georgian. When they were in my bedroom, pulling at my limbs and trying to subdue me, I only knew that they sounded like they were from somewhere far away. And my mind, foggy from whatever was beginning to happen inside of me, thought that perhaps this meant they had the wrong person. That I could talk my way out of this, like I'd done in so many other situations.

We were in a weird sort of dance, with the comforter caught between me, still in my pajamas, and this man dressed all in black, his face covered in a mask like you'd see in a spy movie. I'd move left, fighting the pull of my body to give up, and he'd move right and grip harder. I'd try to slip through, and his arms would tighten around my shoulders with the curved edge of the gun pressed more firmly into my temple.

Afterwards the doctors at the hospital would have to sew three stitches there, from the tension tearing at my skin.

The FBI said that's what made them think this was perhaps their first job. They were overzealous, passionate.

I heard that and decided the exact opposite. Maybe these men just really wanted me dead.

We started moving from the bedroom and out into the hallway. I spotted two other men, armed with guns and masks like my dancing partner, who were stationed outside the bedroom door.

I was still very weak, despite all the adrenaline kicking through my system. In the back of my mind was a growing fear that if I didn't die today from these men then I might be already dying. I knew, underneath my terror, that something was happening to me and I couldn't control it.

In the moment though, I had to focus on what was most important: I needed to keep my family safe. So I gathered the strength I still had and screamed out into the lavender-scented air of the mansion my wife and I had rebuilt. I screamed as loud as I could, and as hard as my lungs would let me.

"Get out!" I told my family. "Get. Out!"

The men said something between each other that I couldn't understand, and the one holding me called into a walkie-talkie he had strapped to his chest. At this point we'd dropped the comforter somewhere along the hallway, and our two bodies were pressed even more tightly together. My legs wouldn't hold me up, and so he had to hoist me over his hip with one hand and level the barrel of the gun at my head with the other. He smelled like garlic and pickled onion, and I gagged at the back of my throat.

The result was exactly what I'd hoped wouldn't happen. Brenna turned the corner from the front stairwell, running as quickly as her stiletto heels would allow her. She was holding a cup of tea, probably meant for me, which she promptly dropped as she ran towards us.

That's my wife. Always running towards disasters.

The cup made a sharp pop as it hit the floor, followed by the shower of tinkling pieces as it shattered.

Brenna stopped on the stairs, her hands up in surrender.

The man holding me turned reflexively towards the sound, and I tried to slip from his grasp, maybe grab at his gun, but I didn't have the chance.

The pressure on me released, and there was the soft crumple of a body hitting the floor and then two more loud pops from the opposite direction.

Brenna screamed as the men around me fell and I stayed standing. Wobbly and weak, but still alive.

Tobias showed himself first, emerging from the shadows of the west wing with a shot gun still poised in the air. Darren came from the opposite side, a handgun hanging from his side.

Then the door to Daphne's room opened and her bright head of curls popped out. "I called 911," her tiny voice said, echoing down the hallway like she was asking for a snack after school.

Brenna rushed forward and caught me as I stumbled, almost falling down the stairs.

"Get back in your room," she half-ordered, half-pleaded to our daughter.

Sirens began to sound in the distance a few seconds later, and another minute or two after that our family home was flooded with police and tactical forces and, then later, with cheap-suited detectives.

I was rushed to the hospital, Brenna holding my hand.

That's when we learned that there was something else wrong with me besides my business choices. Besides my success, at all cost, mentality.

That's when Brenna insisted we put in the security measures.

It's when I insisted we buy a gun, for ourselves.

Because, up until the point where they killed the men attacking us, I had no idea the men who worked in and outside my home every day had weapons hidden at Granfield Manor.

Because, I also knew there was no way the police could have arrived there as quickly as they did. Not unless someone had called much earlier than Daphne said she did.

Something was very wrong in my home. Something still is.

And now I'm finally getting close to figuring out exactly what that something is.

31

FELIX

Darren's apartment smells like French fries and stale air. It's the kind of apartment where the door opens onto a stairwell, and you climb up it in order to get to the actual living space above. I take the stairs two at a time, and it feels like I have an extra five inches on my legs as I pop up with each step I take. Another book I read, on physiology and anatomy, says that I'm the prime age for growth spurts of biological males—I'll be putting on a lot of muscle soon.

By the time we go back to school, whenever that's going to be, my classmates won't recognize me. Maybe I'll actually look like my dad, rather than just having my mom say that I do.

The mask I'm wearing itches on my face, and I have to fight the urge to tug at it. Whenever I get online, every site I go to is blaring the same messages. Wash your hands. Don't touch your face. Stay away from people.

The gloves I'm wearing are fine, but the gown seems built for someone much larger than me in the shoulders. It flops around my chest like I'm wrapped in a blanket.

I'll have to burn these afterwards.

Darren's apartment doesn't have much in it. There's a bed in the corner, a little kitchenette to the left with a normal-sized fridge, a tiny stove, and some cabinets. A chair and bookcase are at right angles in the opposite corner. There's a door leading off the kitchen, which I assume is the bathroom, and a closet sunk into the wall by the bed. I have other things that I need to do, but I can't help myself. I walk over to the bookcase and read the spines.

Viruses don't last on paper. Not for long, at least.

Most of the titles are Ernest Hemingway or those huge fantasy books that everyone's making TV shows or movies out of. No textbooks. No gardening books either. A few are written in a different kind of alphabet I can't read.

Okay, I have to refocus. I don't have much time, and this needs to be done.

The bed is made tight, with hospital corners and a small pillow fluffed at the head of it. I don't want to mess up the neatness of it all, but I need to do this. I reach underneath the mattress and pull. It's heavier than I expected—our mattresses are really light because they're made of that new astronaut material, which makes them perfect for hiding stuff inside with a little sewn patch to cover it. I have to pull up twice before I'm able to get a look under it.

The sun passes behind a cloud for a moment and the apartment gets dark really quickly. Below the mattress is a big pool of black shadow. I'm tempted to turn on the light, but I can't have anyone know I'm here, obviously.

I wait for my eyes to adjust to the change, and as I do I hear something rattle from the kitchen. I turn my head, the mattress still lifted in my arms, and listen harder.

There it is again. It's definitely metal against metal. But now it's more of a scratching than a rattle. Like something hard moving against something harder, not small pieces jumbled up together.

I scan under the mattress now I can see clearly in the darkness, but there's nothing there, so I put it down and go through the tiny kitchen to the bathroom door. It's closed, but when I pull at the knob it opens easily. The smell of damp air hits me like a wave, and steam rises up, clouding the air.

There's a window above the toilet, and it only takes a few moments for the air to clear once I open it. Glancing around the small space, I realize what the sound I heard was. The hot water handle on the sink is loose, and swings back and forth against its bearing. Water turns on and off as the handle swings. When I take a step towards it, the handle shifts back and water gushes out. Little swirls of steam rise up from the water as it pours down the drain.

Weird, I think.

Not just because the sink is broken in a way that seems odd, but because everything else in Darren's apartment is so neat and organized. It doesn't seem like he'd leave anything broken for long.

I go back out into the kitchen and rummage around in the drawers until I find a rubber band. Back in the bathroom, I do a quick adjustment with the band around the handle and the scratching and wobbling stops.

If only Mom could see me now, being so capable and bright. I feel like she looks at me differently since everything that happened at the school. Peanut butter. It had to be stupid peanut butter.

Of course, Daphne loves the stuff.

Before I can stop myself I open the few cabinets in Darren's kitchen, searching. I find instant coffee, bags of rice and a few sugar and salt packets mixed in with canned soup. And then, hidden behind cans of tuna, there it is. A jumbo size generic container of peanut butter.

Margot's allergic to it. I haven't forgotten that. In fact, it's why I grabbed at it in the first place.

And then, behind the peanut butter, I find what I came here for.

It's not hidden underneath the mattress, like I'd expected. Someone has shoved it in the pantry. Hidden in plain sight.

Dad insisted that Darren have a key card. I overheard Mom and him arguing about it one night, when Dad could still shout. She didn't think the outdoor employees should be able to get to Dad, and then he'd asked Mom where they'd all be if Darren hadn't been able to get into the house that night. Mom didn't have a reply to that.

I grab the key card and slip it through the gap in the gown and into the back pocket of my jeans.

I think someone's been visiting Dad. Someone who isn't supposed to. I've been thinking more and more about what he said the day Margot fell off the horse—how "they're coming". What if he isn't imagining things? What if someone else figured out how to break-in to his rooms, like I did?

Each key card keeps a record of when it's used, and I know how to get the report right off my laptop, since I downloaded a copy of the security software back when it was first installed. Dad couldn't protect us, and Mom was gone so often. I figured it was up to me.

Now I can see who's been using Darren's card.

It doesn't occur to me until after I'm out of the apartment, I've burnt my "protective equipment" in the pit of the original bonfire from our panic room night, and I'm heading back to the house like some outdoorsy kid ready for a snack, that keeping the key card in Darren's apartment doesn't make any sense. Why wouldn't the person leave it hidden somewhere inside the house? It'd be more obvious they were doing something wrong if they were caught going in and out of Darren's apartment, rather than someone finding a key card on them.

I don't normally feel stupid, but when I feel the pressure on the back of my neck, followed by a quick and searing pain spread out into my shoulders and then blackness, I have a few seconds of total, utter despair that I'm the stupidest boy who'd ever lived.

32

TOBIAS

The horses smell the burning glass and metal before I do. Of course they do.

I run around the stable first, checking that somehow the hay or the spare planks stacked for repairs hadn't spontaneously caught fire. Thinking of the dead fox I found, I also wanted to make sure no one had set a fire inside.

Between the hay, feed, and wood stalls the stables are essentially a tinder box.

Colleen was afraid of horses, which is partly why I stopped riding and going to the stables when we were married. She was convinced I'd fall off and become paralyzed, like a famous movie star-turned-paraplegic-turned-activist. I used to think it was really kind of sweet and loving, how she worried so much about me falling and getting hurt. I was happy to give it up for her.

But then I realized, after I walked those leftover meatballs over to the guy who was banging my wife, that maybe she wasn't really focused on trying to protect me, so much, as trying to protect herself.

You can't leave a husband who suddenly finds himself

disabled, can you? Also, you don't really have time for secret trysts in your marital bed if your actual husband is bedridden.

The prison they sent me to, which was really more of a psychiatric clinic with bars—imagine my luck at finding the one system in the state that actually provided real mental health care for inmates—well, it had a whole therapeutic horseback-riding program. Equine therapy.

So that's where I learned how to love again. It just didn't involve people.

All my searching tells me that my horses are safe. But they're not happy.

Jasmine's eyes roll to the side of her head and she rears up slightly as I get closer to her stall. I grip her bridle and stroke the long side of her jaw, and she calms enough to stand still. I whisper into her velvet ear that I'll be back. That she'll be safe.

Don't worry, I tell all my charges, their soft liquid eyes looking back at me with the most magnificent trust. I'll keep you safe.

I close the stable door behind me, and walk out into a drifting cloud of gray smoke. It smells like chemicals, different from the other fires we've had burning at Granfield recently.

Over the tops of the trees blocking the main house from the greenhouse there's a funnel of smoke spewing up into the sky. A sharp crack of glass shrieks through the air, followed by clattering metal.

I take off running as fast as I can, and on the path to the trees and the fire I hear a door slam and footsteps coming from the house. I don't waste time turning to look, and soon enough Brenna is holding pace with me. Her hair flies in the wind and she's a blur of well-cut navy wool and cream silk. Her steps make an odd slap on the ground each time they touch, and I realize with a slight jolt that she's barefoot.

That's not going to help, I think.

When we arrive through the copse of trees the heat of the fire makes a wall that we can't get past. Brenna and I exchange looks, and nodding wordlessly with each other I move behind one of the closest trees and try to navigate to the far side of the greenhouse where the rain barrels are stored. If they're not already melted down, this will be the closest source of water we can use to try to put the fire out.

Brenna shifts to the other side, both of us staying on the far perimeter of the fire's reach, since neither of us can push past the forcefield of heat. There's a rustling in the trees to my left, but I don't wait to see which animal is escaping. I force myself to move forward. The air is charred and full of debris, so I pull the collar of my flannel shirt up over my mouth, hoping to filter out some of the toxins from the air.

I'm really glad I closed the stable doors. None of this would be good for the horses.

I don't even try the rain barrels close to the greenhouse. I head straight for the backup barrels lined up neatly along the machine-shed wall.

Brenna runs to the stream, where Darren had set up a bilge pump several years ago that was meant to help divert the water if the level of the stream and connected lake at the front of the house rose too high after big rains. They were having trouble with the ground flooding, and the lawn of the main house was getting too soggy and unpleasant for evening walks. I remember it was Mark's idea, because he liked to walk around Granfield in the evenings, before he got sick.

If Brenna can switch on the pump and direct it towards the greenhouse, she might be able to staunch the fire before it catches the forest line. I've already assumed that the copse of trees around the greenhouse is going to burn. There's no stopping it.

The rain barrels are full after several days of recent spring rain, so I have to really heave against them in order to manage to tip the first, and then the second, over. The water inside sloshes back and forth and the barrel almost walks itself on its side, like a drunk falling over but still insisting on dancing to some silent tune.

I dig my heels into the dirt, and push with all my strength again the hard plastic side. I need to get it aligned with the road, so that the water will release into the path of the fire and hopefully put it out before it spreads to the other buildings on the grounds.

The fire thunders in my ears. So loud it sounds mechanical. Manmade and deadly. The heat and the sound combine together and plow through the air, like a freight train aiming straight for Granfield.

I remember that sound. I remember needing to fight against the push of the heat and the natural instinct to run as far away from the flames as I possibly could.

But I didn't. Colleen was inside our house, and the walls were dripping with flames. I heard her crying out my name, and so I didn't hesitate. I rushed in. No tools, no plan.

I went in to save my wife. And the baby.

I knew at that point that it probably wasn't *my* baby.

I searched and searched, but the flames were too high by then. They were supposed to be smaller, more contained. The way our home was built, though, was different from older houses I knew. Ours was built like a matchstick house, with cheap boards in the floor joints caddy-corner to each other. Builders actually call them matchstick houses now.

And they build them anyway.

At the trial the prosecutor said I have a sort of hero complex. That's why I ran into the burning building instead of calling for help. That's why having Colleen cheat on me was so damaging to my ego. That's why Colleen died.

Only some of that is true.

None of it mattered in the end, because Colleen was still dead.

Fire licks the sky. I uncap the barrels and let the water flow over the dirt path and into the ravine of the greenhouse's foundation, and the field beyond. The water evaporates before it even makes it to the lower fields. Steam rushes out of the fire, and a cloud of fog and smoke surrounds Granfield.

I could slip away now, and no one would know I'd left. I realize that.

I could probably live out in the woods for a time. I learned how to do that when I was a kid, going camping with my parents. Staying out late in the night with my friends, drinking by the bonfire. I have some money saved, stashed away in a bank that's online and doesn't ask a lot of questions. I live a pretty simple life, and the Stones pay well, so over the years I've accumulated a good chunk of savings.

There won't be enough food now, for Granfield. We've lost everything we've been growing.

So that means that I *have* to stay. Someone has to protect the horses. Someone has to do the right thing.

I don't stay to watch the fire consume what's left of the greenhouse. I leave Brenna to mess with the bilge pumps, knowing they won't help. The fire's too far gone, and everything around the greenhouse is going to burn.

Instead, I walk back to the stable. I would pull up the loose board where I kept the shotgun, but after the night Mark was almost kidnapped Brenna told me it needed to go. She said I'd saved her husband, and she was so very grateful, but that it wasn't okay that I'd kept a weapon at Granfield without telling them. What if Felix or Daphne had found it?

Fair enough, I thought, so I got rid of it.

I find a comfortable stool and tip it back against Jasmine's stall door, so I have a clear view of the door. I've got my shovel next to me, hiding in plain sight. It could kill a man as easily as a gun, if you know how to use it right.

Jasmine nuzzles my neck with her soft whiskery lips, and I shush her and feed her one of the last sugar cubes from the box.

33

DAPHNE

Nobody likes a tattletale. That's what Veronica said at school one day when I told Mrs. Kilpatrick somebody was stealing snacks from the snack cart by her desk.

But I didn't care. I just didn't want to watch poor Tommy Winger stare at the pile of goldfish crackers on his desk anymore. He'd wait for a few seconds, and then he'd shove them all in his mouth in one swoop, while stupid Veronica would eat hers like she was the queen of something. One piece at a time.

I asked Mom about Tommy once, and if we could have him over for dinner, but she said that his parents probably wouldn't like that. They were both working a lot and Tommy lived with his grandmother and somehow I guess other parents for the school gave their own money so that he could go to school with us. Which seems weird, because can't anybody go to school anywhere they want?

Isn't that why I had to deal with Veronica and her friends treating everyone like we were their servants. If we're able to pick who goes to different schools, then why would anyone pick someone so mean?

I'm glad I don't have to see Veronica anymore. I hope I never have to see her again.

Sometimes when I'd play with Teddy, and now with my other dolls, I pretend one of them is Tommy and then I put all the fancy cakes and cookies in my tea set in front of him and he gets to eat them all and take his time. He doesn't have to rush through, worrying that another kid is going to take his treat.

Lately I've been feeling a little like Tommy.

I went outside this afternoon to try to get my mind off my growling tummy. Mom's keeping track of all the food in the house, and we're not allowed to get anything to eat unless she approves of it first.

She's excited about the vegetables in the greenhouse. She keeps talking about how Tobias is going to save us with the garden they've planted, but I'm not so sure. If I don't like Veronica, then I absolutely hate vegetables.

And I can't find the peanut butter. Mom's stashed it somewhere out of reach.

Anyway, I went outside to try to stop thinking about how hungry I was and I heard someone around the corner from the stables. I thought it might be Tobias and that he was taking one of the horses out, so I rushed over to see and maybe pet them a bit, but when I got there nobody was around.

It's weird, because I really thought I heard someone on the gravel. That's the thing about gravel. It crunches under your feet, like Rice Krispies. Oh, I could eat a whole box of Rice Krispies. Mom made me eat beans for breakfast. I almost threw them up, but I didn't because I'm so hungry.

After looking around the stables—the horses were there, all cozied up, and Tobias wasn't anywhere around—I walked over to the greenhouse to see what I would have to eat soon. I didn't have to go far though, to realize what had happened.

The closer I got to the greenhouse the more the air smelled

like a bonfire. I didn't think anything was wrong at first, because it seems like these days Mom and Margot and whoever else are always burning things in the fire pit, but this smelled different. It was stronger.

And I swear, the closer I got to the greenhouse the hotter it felt. It was sunny, and I was wearing my hat like Mom always tells me to, because I have to protect my skin and "I'll thank her when I'm older", but this was different. It was like being too close to the fireplace in the library where Mom likes to work now.

I didn't see the fire until I got past the group of trees by the greenhouse where I like to play sometimes. There are all sorts of nice hiding places underneath the tree branches, and I'm tiny enough that I can spend hours and hours there pretending I'm somewhere else.

After I came through the clearing though, the heat was more than just a fireplace. It was like being hit by something hard and hot. *Whoomp*, it smacked into me and I stumbled a little bit and cut my ankle on one of the paving stones.

I had to back away, because the entire greenhouse was on fire. And it wasn't just the glass building. All the ground around it was burning, too. It was like something out of a movie.

The smoke was getting really bad, and my ankle really hurt but I knew that if I stayed there I would get hurt even more. I wanted to call out to Mom or Felix, but there was this roaring sound that was getting louder and louder and I didn't think I could make my voice loud enough for anyone to hear me over that huge roar.

So I went and hid underneath one of the trees. It was still cool underneath the branches, and so I hid until the roaring stopped.

I hid while other people came and screamed at the fire. I

stayed there, without anyone noticing me, while Mom and Tobias tried to put the fire out.

Maybe I should have gone and gotten help, but I don't like vegetables and this way Mom will have to let me eat the peanut butter. Plus, I was really scared. Any kid would be, wouldn't they?

That's what I'm counting on everyone thinking.

Before Mom and everyone else came to try to save the greenhouse, I saw something else. Something really important. Something that could help everyone figure out why the greenhouse burnt down.

The thing I didn't tell Veronica that day in school was that I told on her for another reason. It wasn't just to help Tommy make sure he had enough to eat and that he could enjoy his snack. I told on her because I was sick and tired of not getting enough fun snacks either. At home, Greta always refused to buy anything like goldfish crackers or fruit snacks or even potato chips. School was the only place I could get the special treats I wanted.

When I want something, I usually get it.

So this time I'm not going to be a tattletale. I'll let them figure it out all alone.

34

MARK

I wake, strapped into my bed again. It's a surreal feeling, to be restrained in your own home, in your own bed, by the people you love because they think you're going to hurt yourself.

If I were smarter, I'd learn how to play the game and make sure they didn't worry about me, but it's so hard sometimes, with the weight of the day pressing down on you like a thousand pounds of water. And then you come up to the surface and you can barely breathe, sick with the bends.

The light from the small lamp in the corner of the adjacent room dances along the ceiling in the darkness.

"Who's there?"

No one responds to my question. I try to move my arms and legs, but whoever has done the straps secured them tight. Sometimes, when Felix is asked to do it he'll leave enough space around the buckles to let me slip out and find some relief.

"Can you untie me?" I'm certain someone is there. I can hear their breathing, even over the timid blip and hum of the machines Brenna insists I stay hooked up to.

The person in the corner moves further into the edge of my

sick room until I can't see them anymore. Oh, how easy it is for some people to disappear.

When I first started my company, I was going to change the world. For the better, I should add. I was going to make people's lives *better* with my technology. Alternative energy is the future —I still believe that, by the way, not that it seems to matter now —and fifteen years ago I came out of school with venture capitalists frothing at the mouth to give me their money so I could expand solar panel use and installation. I'd come up with a way to capture solar energy that was almost three times as efficient as the best product out there, and everybody wanted in.

So I set up a company and got funding. I hired a lawyer and some programmers and other executive-type people, who got the factory in China up and running, and I'd made my first million clear of costs and overhead within six months. It was a success, and it was making energy more available to everyone, across the world.

I felt like a real hero.

I met Brenna in college when we were both undergrads. It was wild at first, to be with someone so beautiful and smart and absolutely ruthless. It was different from anything else I'd ever experienced, and she opened my eyes to all sorts of new possibilities, just when I thought my life was over.

I may have built a billion-dollar company, but Brenna did almost the same thing in about half the time. I never questioned how she did it, and by the time it was too late, and I had a gun to my head after being ripped from a fucking hospital bed in my own home, I didn't even want to know.

Sure, people think those hired guns who broke into our home were there for me, and I suppose they were in a way, but it's my wife who's the killer. She sees an opportunity, and nothing will stop her from getting exactly what she wants.

I saw it in her face, that night when the men came and

ripped me from my bed and waved guns around my home. Brenna was frightened. There was no mistaking that.

In her own way, I know she loves me. And the children. But when she looked at me that night, there was something missing from her face. The way she set her jaw. The cool leveling of her eyes at mine.

She wasn't going to give up her life to save mine. And by her life, I mean her company. Her real baby she's brought into this world. She was going to negotiate some sort of truce with whoever hired those men. But first she was going to let them shoot me. I saw it in her face.

But then Darren and Tobias rescued me.

I'm thinking all of this now, as though it was something I had figured out in that slice of a moment between being alive and being dead on the stairwell, but I didn't. Afterwards, I was just so relieved to be alive, and that my family had survived, that I wasn't thinking about Brenna and what she did. Or didn't do. It's not until now, my head finally clearing, that I'm able to ask that essential question: *Why? Why did she want me dead?*

Afterwards we bought a gun and Brenna put in the keypads and the extra locks, while I got sicker and sicker. I was fighting for my life and trying to run my company, and all the while Brenna was taking away my lifelines, slowly and steadily, until I wouldn't have anything left to keep me connected to the outside world.

My ability to move, my ability to speak. Surrounded by loved ones, but no one who would listen to me.

No, it was only after all these months and months of lying in this bed that I realized what Brenna was doing. My mind's gotten clearer and the edges sharper.

That's why she fired the nurse that was here before Margot. She was starting to pay attention to what I said—not just understand it, but really listen to it—and Brenna couldn't have that.

I know Margot's been hurt, but I'm not sure how badly. She hasn't been to see me for days and days.

Tobias has told me things, while sitting here at my bedside, that have made my blood cool. Terrible things.

"Are you still there?"

I try one more time, but whoever was in here watching me has gone. I'm alone, in this darkened room, unable to protect myself with anything other than my thoughts.

I hear a door slam, somewhere far away—over in the other wing of the house, I'm sure—and I picture Margot's kind face, looking down at me as she held my hand.

I wonder if she'll live to see the end of this.

35

BRENNA

"I don't know what to do." I squeeze Mark's hand. It's early morning, and the medicine we give him at night ensures that he sleeps deeply. He can't hear me, but that's okay. I don't know if I want him to hear this.

"We are all going to die if I don't do something," I continue.

Tobias keeps saying that the greenhouse probably caught on fire naturally. There were a lot of chemicals stored in there, he said, and all I wanted to do was scream at him, "Well, then why did you keep them all there, together?" If they were so easy to go up in flames, why didn't you do something to protect us?

I fed the children more beans for dinner tonight. Beans every meal of the day now, until the end of time. I've had to soak them overnight, and then boil them into a mush the next day. We have bags and bags of them, thanks to Greta doing some online ordering in bulk from a natural foods website Mark had turned her onto a while ago. I'd never heard of it before, but Mark knew—knows—all of those companies from his own business connections. NatureFill, the bags say. Mark probably went to lunch with the CEO and then decided to order a bunch of products after hearing the company's pitch. That's just the type of guy he is—the kind who invests in a company before knowing anything more about it except that he likes their talk and that they paid for lunch. He listens to his gut.

And sometimes his gut pays off, and sometimes it loses.

I get up and move over to the safe buried at the back of the linen closet. Everything is locked up tight in this house, but I know that doesn't really matter. If someone wants to get in bad enough, they'll get in.

And then there are the people who are already inside these walls, or on these grounds. I think of that altar underneath the tree, the blood smeared across the doll's face. Margot looked so scared when I told her.

Behind me, Mark stirs in his sleep. He's looking worse and worse. His skin is waxy and he keeps losing weight. I've had to increase some of the dosages for his painkillers, just to keep him from trying to leave the bed and screaming out in his sleep.

It won't be long now. And when he goes, what will I have left?

Felix and Daphne.

Being a mother is so hard. Loving your children is hard. You're supposed to give them everything you have, and they still grow and change until they're unrecognizable from the image you had of them in your head when you first held them. They do things that are stupid or cruel or embarrassing, but that bond between the two of you is supposed to help you through it. To be unbreakable.

You end up doing things for your children you thought you'd never be capable of.

I pull the gun out and check that the safety is on before tucking it back into my waistband and covering it with the expensive silk shirt I optimistically wore today, which is now singed and scarred with black streaks from the fire. When I get dressed in the morning, if I look in the mirror, my ribs protrude out like a set of jewels inlaid in a casket.

Death is all around me. I see it everywhere.

When I leave Mark's corner of Granfield Manor I close the door as quietly as I can and wait for the heaviness on my shoulders to lift. It's easier to pretend everything is okay when you're not watching your husband waste away.

There's a rustling in the hall, somewhere down towards Margot's room, which she's still in. Tobias and I never moved her in with Mark. Tobias disappeared in the middle of the greenhouse burning, probably thinking of his dead wife, and I couldn't face looking for him. The only thing I could do was let what had just happened sink in, and try to sort through it all. So Margot is staying right where she is.

The rustling comes again, and I walk down the hallway towards the library room I've converted into an office. The door is ajar and someone is inside, moving things around.

There's a scrape of a chair against the reclaimed wood floor and the heavy scratch of a drawer opening in the desk. I swear that when I listen at night to the damp softness of this exquisitely expensive house, I can hear the whisper of book pages being turned.

I wait, hoping to catch whoever is invading my personal space in the act. Felix has come banging around before, trying to get in. He didn't come out with the fire to help, and I haven't gone looking for him since. I have no clue where my son is, I realize.

I reach back and feel the hard skeleton of the gun in my palm. You can never be too careful when you're the only one in your family who realizes what's really happening.

I creep closer to the door, push it open with the palm of my free hand, and let the scene in front of me sink in.

There they are, sitting in my chair, trying to take over my life and put me out of my misery at the same time.

I hold the gun out, not a tremble in my arm—not even in the slightest—and poise my finger on the trigger. The pale blue of the computer screen gives their shoulders and chin an eerie glow, like they're being lit from within.

On the screen is the image of another person, looking out into our world. Dressed in black, a thick accent coloring their words as they bark out instructions across the feeble internet connection.

"It will cost you," the man in the screen says. "Are you willing to pay our price?"

The figure in front of me nods in the affirmative, and starts to explain how they'll get their hands on the money. I creep in further, and that's when the man in the screen looks up. He sees me, and the gun, but fear doesn't cross his face. Just a firm resignation.

"Looks like you have bigger problems," he says through lips that flatten into two rigid lines. His screen clicks off, and the glow turns to blackness.

My adversary turns around in the chair, and it's when I see their eyes ripe with fear that a tremble creeps into my grip.

"I can explain," they say. "It's not what it seems."

Of course, I don't believe them. But I do hesitate, like some amateur, and that's all it takes for them to move on me and strip the gun away.

"Are you listening?" they ask, my gun pointed straight at my head.

36

FELIX

I wake in my room. My head throbs like someone's bouncing a kick ball against my right ear. The covers are pulled up to my chin, and I have to wriggle my arms around in order to get out of the tight sheets.

As soon as I'm free, I jump out of bed. I need to get to Mom, or Daphne. Dad needs me.

But I feel sick all of a sudden and have to grip at the table by my bed. Then I throw up onto the floor, which is just as awful as it sounds. The room spins around me. They must have hit me harder than I realized.

Which means that they could do even worse to everyone else in the house. I slither across the floor towards my bedroom door. I hold on to the doorframe and try to pull myself up the side. My palms are sweaty from puberty or the concussion, or both, and my hands slip on the smooth wood.

I'm a mess. Dad would be so disgusted with me.

So would Mom.

I take a deep breath and try to focus my eyes on a point in the distance. I can do this.

When I step through the door I'm hit with a smell I don't

recognize. Tangy and metallic, like licking a battery that's been supercharged. Whatever it is pricks at my spine, and the wooziness I felt a few moments ago is replaced with bright bursts of fear tracking through my nervous system.

Because it's blood. Of course, it's blood.

37

DAPHNE

I hate Margot.

I hate her so much.

That's what I want to scream into everyone's faces, but instead I came to see the horses. I like them. They don't make me do things I don't want to do. They never talk about me behind my back, or bring weird women into the house who want to watch me play with my toys. And, most important of all, they don't kiss my mother when they're not supposed to.

Even though I'm short and maybe I have to go to bed early or else I start to get really cranky, I know about things.

Jasmine tucks her head down from her stall and nuzzles my right ear. She can tell when I'm upset. That's another reason I like the horses. They know when you aren't feeling like yourself, or when you're worried or upset. Jasmine and Julie do a better job than most of my family does.

My stomach growls. I'm not hungry though. All Mom has been feeding us are beans and lentils and then beans again. My stomach feels like a balloon that's going to burst.

Jasmine's huge horse lips snuffle against my cheek and I turn to scratch her behind her right ear. That's her favorite place. I hear Julie and the other horses shifting in their stalls.

"I'll come pet all of you, don't worry," I tell them. I'd do it even if I had a lot of homework or chores or whatever to do, but I'll especially be careful and get each spot for them because there's nothing else to do.

My tummy makes another weird sound. Ugh, it hurts. I have to stop petting Jasmine and grab ahold of my stomach and bend over a little.

Maybe peanut butter sandwiches don't mix with beans? I think.

I'd found the jar Mom stashed away after she caught me being rude to Margot that one day during breakfast. The strange thing is that I liked Margot for a long time. I even had a doll that kind of looked like her, and I would have her—the doll—sit at my table and pretend to have tea with all of my other stuffed animals. But then the doll went missing, or maybe I left it under the trees where I like to play, and I had to replace it with something else. Margot was nice and she took care of my dad really well. She wore these cool uniforms with different animals on them sometimes, and when I asked she'd let me listen to my heartbeat with her stethoscope. But then one night I had a nightmare and I went to Mom's bedroom and Mom wasn't there.

I was going to go get Felix instead, but his stupid door was locked again, so I decided that Margot would be able to help. That's when I found out about them, about my mom and the nurse. Apparently that's almost as clichéd—I learned that word from Greta when she'd let me sit in the kitchen while she made dinner and watched her shows on the television—anyway, it's almost as clichéd as Dad having an affair with the nanny, which we don't have because Mom wants people to think she's a superhero or something. Superwoman. I heard Greta say that too once.

"What are you doing here?"

Tobias startles me out of my tummy ache for a moment. He's coming down from the hay loft that you can climb into from the back side of the stables. I keep my arms wrapped around my belly as I watch him, and the horses all move in their stalls because they know I don't feel well. He was so quick to help me when this all began. I didn't even have a chance to tell him to stop and to unwrap that awful blanket from my face. It smelled like the horses, but also like wild animals and poo and stinky breath, and it scratched at my face like the wool sweaters Mom makes me wear for the family pictures she has us take every year.

"I was just petting the horses."

"What's wrong with you?" He doesn't come near me though. Not like last time.

Something's different.

Jasmine whinnies behind me.

"Shush, girl. That's a good girl," Tobias says, but the way he says it seems to only make the horses more nervous.

"I have a tummy ache," I tell him. "I don't feel so good."

I get that feeling where you know you're going to throw up. I glance around, trying to see if there's a bucket anywhere for me to use, and grab one sitting next to Jasmine's stall. It's full of oats though, and as I pull it towards me I know that I'm not going to be able to stop myself. Up comes all those beans Mom made me eat for breakfast, and the peanut butter sandwich I made with the two little ends of bread that I found inside a cake box in the cupboard, and the juice I drank with it.

"No!" Tobias shouts. "What are you doing?"

He rushes up to me and yanks at the bucket, but I have a really hard grip on it and I can't seem to let go.

The oats are ruined. My tummy feels better, but I know what I've done.

Julie gives a stomp on the ground with her hoof, and Tobias moves away from me again.

"Get out," he says, not looking at me.

I wipe my mouth with the back of my hand because I don't have anything else and my mouth feels wet and gross. I set the bucket down by my feet.

"I'm sorry," I tell him, and Jasmine and Julie. "I really don't feel good."

"Go lie down then," Tobias says to the stable wall. All I can see is his back, and the skin of his neck has gotten really red.

There's nothing I can do, so I stand up and walk really carefully out of the stable, making sure not to bump into anything or to ruin anything else.

The air feels cold on my face as I go through the open stable doors, and I spot a tall patch of grass out in the distance, by the field, that looks really comfortable.

I don't want to go back into the house yet.

There are clangs and a whooshing sound from the stable behind me, and I think it's Tobias getting rid of my throw-up and the ruined food for the horses. I look out into the field as I sit down on the patch of grass and think that maybe I could find food for them. Horses eat grass and hay, and so maybe I could work really hard and go out into the field and make up for the food I wasted.

But suddenly I'm so tired. My head hurts, although my stomach feels calmer than it did before I spoiled Jasmine's lunch.

I'll lie down here, in the sunshine, for a few minutes, I tell myself. Just long enough for Margot to drink her coffee. I saw Mom get it ready for her this morning. Margot shouldn't be able to taste the peanut butter in it. Greta told me once that coffee is meant to be bitter, and that people drink it after dinner because it hides other flavors they may not like.

I close my eyes, and dream about my family being happy again.

38

MARGOT

There was the hot acidic smell of smoke earlier too, but that's faded away by now.

Brenna and Tobias never came to move me to the other wing of the house. No one has come to see me in a long while, except for Daphne. She brought me a cup of coffee. I couldn't believe we still had some left. I was so glad to see someone at first that I reached out to hold her hand when she set the tray down next to the bed. She didn't let me touch her though, and after a moment I remembered that there's a doll under a tree, somewhere outside, that looks like me and that's smeared with something's blood.

She stepped away from me and before either of us could get more uncomfortable she left, promising that her mom would be back to check on me soon.

My ribs ache through my back and just breathing is still difficult. Tobias changed the wrapping around my chest yesterday, and it's loosened now and needs to be redone in order to give me a decent amount of support so that I can stand up without feeling like I'm dying.

A door slams, and angry voices cut through the walls.

The window. I can make it to the window.

I'm wearing my normal pajamas—a large white men's T-shirt and soft cotton boxer shorts—and they both hang loosely around me. I sniff at my shirt as I shift to stand up, and the smell of unwashed skin and body-warmed sheets mingles with the aroma of the coffee Daphne brought for me. I take a sip, grateful for the caffeine and that the act of reaching out to hold the cup isn't as painful as I thought it would be, before trying to move the rest of my body out of bed.

The only other bone I've broken in my entire life was when Mom forgot to pick me up from school after soccer practice and I decided to walk the three miles home, and managed to get clipped by a pickup truck going way too fast on the side road I was walking down. Broken femur. I lay in the ditch by the side of the road for almost two hours before Teresa found me when she started searching the likely routes I'd take home. She took me to the hospital, helped me with my cast, and brought me back home. My mom never left her room, the entire time. That's when I really knew she wasn't going to get better. Something inside her was broken, and there wasn't a sturdy cast and some crutches that were going to help her heal, like me.

It was watching Teresa take care of me and of Mom at the same time that made me want to be a nurse. Teresa, of course, went into business, even though she'd have been a great nurse. That's why I found Mark Stone, after all—because of my oldest sister.

I need to do something, not just sip at my coffee like some lady who lunches convalescing in her bedroom.

I take a deep breath as gently as I can and hoist myself up from the bed. Steady on, and here I go. I tug at the wrappings around my chest to tighten them, and I manage to make it all the way to the window without too much searing pain shooting up my sides. Outside, the sky is clear with the sun brightening everything with a golden glow. Mark's wing of the house is straight ahead, and fields stretch out towards the back. The stables cut into the right corner of my view, but not enough for me to see the entrance.

At first I think that no one is outside, but then I spot a small figure in the bright green grass near the back fields. I have to squint, and just the movement of tightening those muscles in my face sends a bright pain through my back, but I'm able to make out Daphne's blond curls and the bright pink shirt she was wearing when she brought the coffee to me.

She looks like she's asleep. I try to watch for movement, because something about the way her arms and legs are splayed out seems not quite right, but it's too far away for me to tell exactly what she's doing or if she's okay.

As I'm turning from the window I spot a flicker of movement in the windows across from me. Someone is moving through Mark's rooms. A reflection gleams off the window for a second, and when I'm able to see inside again the figure is gone.

It didn't look like Brenna—I would have spotted her bright almost-white hair—and Tobias has that fiery red beard that makes him distinctive. Daphne is outside still, and Felix is too short and dark to match who I saw.

Because it was Darren. I'm certain I saw Darren walking into Mark's rooms.

I need to go to him.

I scan the room, grab at a big sweatshirt someone has left limply folded on the chair in the corner, and pull my head through it as gingerly as possible in order to cover my braless chest and thin T-shirt. I can't manage to put pants on, so the boxer shorts will have to do.

Next to the chair in the corner there's a walking stick I've never used, because it always seemed like some decorative artifact Brenna put there to look rustic. I snatch it, place the handle under my armpit, and use it to brace myself. It relieves some of the pressure on my chest, and I'm able to make it through the door and down the hallway faster than I could have anticipated.

I'm so preoccupied with getting to Mark that I don't pay attention to the growing tingling in my lips. My breaths are raspy and getting harder and harder to make, but I'd assumed it was because of my broken ribs.

Too late, I feel my throat start to close and realize I'm not going to make it to Mark. Or Daphne.

Daphne. The doll, the blood. My coffee. What was it that I tasted a hint of as I sipped? I was so focused on the terrible things invading this godforsaken house that I didn't do the most basic thing anyone with a deadly allergy has to do, almost by instinct.

I didn't pay attention to what I was about to put into my body.

My breathing comes in rasps, and my throat tightens like a drumhead. I spin in circles, whirling my arms around me as though that will bring the EpiPen from my room back within reach.

When I collapse on the floor, desperate for air, there's a terrible crack as I drop down against the massive decorative vase in the hallway. And then pain. Waves and waves of pain.

39

DARREN

I slam through the drawers of the medical suite, looking for the correct vial. I know I've seen Brenna and that nurse give Mark doses of the stuff to "calm him down", and even though I prepped things earlier I still can't seem to find it.

My hands shake as I rummage through the supplies. Adrenaline is a hell of a thing.

Brenna looks up at me from the corner of the room where I set her down, hands and feet tied together behind her back. Like an animal.

Not that I think she's an animal, but the woman did try to have me killed because I had a cold. Among other reasons.

She wasn't supposed to see me like that. I was so careful for so long, and now I've ruined it all because I had to use her stupid computer for, of all things, a Skype call. Who knew that even guns for hire needed some sort of verification before they took your money.

Not that I have a lot of it, but Brenna and Mark sure do, which is kind of the point.

Finally, my fingers grip onto the vial I need. Codeine. Perfect.

I find a sterile syringe and rip the packet open, fill the

plunger like I've watched nurses and doctors do on TV a million times, and spritz out a bit at the top to make sure there aren't air bubbles. I glance over at Mark, tied to his bed—talk about treating someone like an animal; I'll untie him as soon as I get everything figured out here—and check he's still sound asleep, in that medication-fogged haze Brenna likes to keep him.

I tied a scarf from the chair of the library around Brenna's mouth, and from her corner she mumbles angrily at me but can't really form any words. I don't give myself a chance to think, I rush over in three quick steps and jam the needle into her arm. It goes in easily, and the drug flows into her so smoothly that I can almost count the seconds—three, two, one—until she's passed out on the floor. I adjust her shoulders and feet so that she's hopefully somewhat comfortable whenever she wakes, which shouldn't be for a while if I estimated the dosage properly, and then stop myself because what the hell do I care that she's comfortable, after what she's done to me. I take the gun from her waistband and slip its cool metal frame against my own side.

I stand at the window, looking out into the courtyard and thinking through what I need to do next. There were footsteps above my head a few minutes ago, which probably means that Felix is awake again. I never wanted to hurt him, but I also couldn't have him taking my key card. I needed to get into this side of the building, not only to check on Mark but to also get supplies.

Daphne's small body is curled up on the soft bed of grass near the further fields. When she was even younger, she'd love to take off her shoes and socks and run through that tussock of grass in her bare feet. She was always such a lovely happy baby.

There's a flash of movement from across the manor house, in the other wing. I see a shock of white and the dark hair framing the nurse's pale face. She was bedridden, with broken ribs.

That day in the forest, I hadn't meant to scare the horses at all. I was out in the woods, near the tree line, trying to clear my head and figure out what I was going to do, when I turned and there they were—the nurse and Tobias, riding our beautiful horses like the world wasn't burning. And I don't know. I guess this wave of anger came up over me, for everything I'd been through, and I couldn't control myself.

I stayed in the shadows and dropped down to my hands and knees, waiting for the right time to spring up and let the horses know that I was there. They say horses can smell fear, but they can also smell anger.

Afterwards, I felt terrible. But there wasn't much I could do to change things.

Just like now.

I scan the room, seeing Brenna sound asleep with a bit of drool dribbling down from the corner of her mouth and Mark still almost frozen in time in his sick bed.

"I'm going to save you," I tell him as I undo his wrist and ankle restraints. I should have done it when I was here earlier, when the greenhouse was burning and the house was empty. I needed to check on the supplies, figure out what was here that I could use. But I couldn't unfasten them, in case someone would guess that I'd been there. Which turned out to be an unnecessary precaution, what with Brenna finding me in her office anyway.

I tuck the gun I took from Brenna in between the mattresses of Mark's bed. I'll get it later. Given what's coming next, it's better to not have a gun on me.

I swipe my key card past the locks on the doors and rush out to where I'm sure Margot is going, after spotting a dead man in her boss's sick room. I'll find her, there's no doubt about that. Like there isn't any doubt about what will happen when I do.

40

FELIX

Counting helps me stay calm, so I count my steps but keep moving towards what I know is going to be awful.

One thousand steps.

That's how many it takes to cross from one end of our home to the other. I know it's strange that it's such an exact number. But there are lots of strange things happening, and the fact that I can walk from our dinner parlor to the end of the kitchen in a perfectly round number seems to be a little less weird than everything else.

But, if that bothers you, I can give you other measurements.

375 seconds. Six minutes and fifteen seconds.

59 breaths.

10 rooms to cross.

25 windows to look out of.

5 people to avoid.

Except today is different. Today, I only get to 785 steps before I see the body.

"Four people to avoid." This new fact slithers out of my mouth before I can replace it with something more appropriate, like "Oh no!" or "Help!" or "Are you okay?" even though I can clearly see that they aren't.

Their pale white fingers clench into a claw that grips at nothing. And there's blood. So, so much blood that I can barely see two eyes blankly staring through the wet curtain of it.

I shouldn't be able to count, but I do and it only takes me 523 steps to run upstairs, past my bedroom and into the panic room. I curl myself into a ball against the soft soundproof walls, pulling my hands over my eyes like a toddler who thinks nobody can see them if they can't see anything themselves.

And that's where I wait for what I know is coming next.

Coming for all of us.

41

TOBIAS

I couldn't kill Darren.

I know I told Brenna that I could. That it was the right choice and that we couldn't risk having the infection spread around, but there's no way for her to understand what it's like to have someone else's life in your hands, and what it means to choose whether they get to go on breathing and eating and loving and making decisions that could hurt other people.

Colleen's affair wasn't the only thing she was hiding from me. Even though she was pregnant, she'd started smoking again. That was something her and our next-door neighbor—Jack—apparently did. *Afterwards.*

My fists clench, thinking of that bastard. Of how he took my life, my love, and my baby all because he couldn't control his stupid urges. Not that Colleen didn't have a choice. She did, and she chose him.

But I can't help believing that we'd still be together, and she'd still be alive, and that I wouldn't be in this hellhole if stupid Jack had been able to keep it in his pants.

She was smoking in bed that night, and she'd get really sleepy all of a sudden sometimes, with the pregnancy. The cigarette was still burning when she fell asleep and she didn't have an ashtray—because she didn't want me knowing what she was doing—and the bed caught on fire in just a few seconds.

I came home from work and smoke was already billowing out of the windows. No one had called it in to 911 yet, and so I had to dial in on my phone while trying to fight against the flames in order to get to my beautiful, pregnant, cheating wife before she burned to death.

I didn't make it, of course. I was too late.

The flames were too big, and the roof of the house was threatening to collapse. The firefighters pulled me out from the wreckage, coughing and blackened by the toxic fumes from our married life burning up around us.

They were trying to get me to sit down in the back of an ambulance while they took my vitals and a separate team of firefighters tried to break through the flames to get to Colleen.

It was over before it began. There was no saving her.

They took me down to the police station, but pretty soon they released me. The fire marshal had already ruled it an accident. They'd found remnants of cigarette smoke, and apparently one of the neighbors was able to tell them that Colleen was a smoker, even though I'd insisted that she wasn't.

Oh, the pity in their eyes when the officers taking my statement looked at me.

That's when I knew. I knew it was fucking Jack Minnigan who'd told them about Colleen, and their affair, and the smoking.

That's when I knew I was going to kill him.

They told me to stay in a hotel that night, and then a social worker would help me find another temporary place to live while insurance and the funeral were worked out. It was all so sterile and bureaucratic.

I vaguely remember calling my mom, and the first words out

of her mouth being, "Did you do it?" I'd been a troubled kid, growing up. But I'd gotten my life straightened out, except Mom was never going to forgive me for what I'd put her through when I was younger.

So I left the hotel they put me up in and I came back home. It smelled like a huge bonfire night, like on the Fourth of July when all the families on a block might get together and cook hotdogs outside on one big fire pit.

It was like a jagged streak running through my mind as I smelled the fire—this thought that part of what I was smelling was Colleen and the baby, drifting on the wind with the ashes.

Jack was standing in front of the house, smoking—of all things. He didn't hear me come up from behind him. I didn't have any weapons on me, not that I had any weapons at that point anyway. So I'd stooped down as I walked over to him and picked up a rock from the edge of the driveway. I remember it was smooth on one side, with a cleaved edge that some sheet of ice probably cracked open a thousand years ago.

I didn't think. Instead, I brought that rock down on Jack's skull, one smooth motion to make him pay for taking my life from me, both before Colleen died and then after too.

But it wasn't that simple. Some instinct perked up in him as I swung and he flinched slightly, enough that the rock smacked into his ear and down his collarbone. He crumpled to the ground, whimpered in pain. I'd assumed it would only take one clean hit to do it.

I hadn't thought I'd have to look him in the eyes as he begged for his life.

Like Darren looked into mine, as Brenna kept barking in the back of my head to *do it, just fucking do it. He needs to die.*

And so I went to prison for assault, not murder.

Because I wanted to have mercy. Because, back then, I wasn't a killer.

42

FELIX

The panic room is so quiet. The walls are soundproofed so anyone screaming from outside, for help or to scare me or to warn me, won't get in. And no one can hear me from inside these walls either.

Not that having people overhear me has ever stopped me from crying like a loser. Like a baby.

My mouth shakes and tears pour down my face. I'm so pathetic. Of course I don't have any friends. Of course my own sister thinks I'm awful, and my parents look at me like I'm a disappointment. Like they wish they'd never had me.

I should have helped her. Instead, I left her there to die, because I was too scared that the same thing would happen to me. That whoever knocked me out when I was coming from Darren's apartment was coming back, to finish what they started.

There's something evil in this house. It keeps growing, day after day. Bigger and crueler. Footsteps on the stairs when no one is there. Wails and moans coming from rooms that are empty. Shadows hanging around outside my door, blocking the hallway light that seeps underneath the crack at night.

Why didn't I help Margot? Because I was scared.

There she was, lying on the floor, covered in blood and grasping at her neck for air, and all I did was run away like a coward.

I bet Daphne would have stayed and held Margot's hand. But Daphne's not here.

I can't stop picturing the way Margot looked when I left her. The unblinking eyes. The grasping hands. I see the broken vase and the blood pooling around her. And then, unwelcome but unstoppable at the same time, my mind zooms in on what I saw. Margot's mouth was open. And her chest, stiff but still moving, if only slightly.

That's when the thought hits me. The certainty of it.

Daphne would have looked longer, and she would have realized what was happening. She would have run to Margot's bedroom and grabbed the EpiPen and stabbed her in the leg with it.

Oh no. Oh my God.

I stop mid-sob, rubbing my hands over my eyes to clear out my vision and run to the door. There's no one on the video monitor. I put in the code, draw in a ragged deep breath, and rush through the door as soon as it opens.

I don't look at my watch, because I can't let myself think I'm too late after that massive pity party I just threw for myself. The layout of the house appears in my mind like a map, and I keep running forward as I consider all the possible routes that I could take to get to Margot's room, get the EpiPen she needs for the allergic reaction she's having, and get to her in as short a span of time as possible.

My heart thrums like a techno beat in my chest, one of those dance songs that never ends that the kids at school blast from their phones at lunch. I can't hear anything over the blood rushing into my brain, muffling all the sounds around me. Or maybe it's the concussion from whatever happened outside earlier.

I take the back stairs, run through the hallway that used to be the servants' hidden entrance, and come out outside Margot's room. It only takes a few seconds, because my legs are longer and I'm flying on adrenaline. My body is pulsing me along.

I can do this, I think.

I can save her.

I don't stop to consider that there are other people in this house. Or other people who might be watching me, waiting for the right moment while I try for once to be the hero.

In Margot's room I know exactly where her medicine is. I'm not proud to say that I snooped around in her bedroom a few times. It was after I'd caught her and Mom kissing, at night in the dark when they thought Daphne and I were asleep. I wanted to know what Margot was like.

I didn't find much. In the table by the bed there was a jumble of coins, a pocketknife, and a framed picture of six women, one of them much older than the other five. They all had dark hair, like Margot. They all looked like Margot, but different enough to seem like they were coming through separate filters on the phone. Wider eyes or pointier chins. All of them were smiling, except for the older woman.

I snatch the EpiPen from underneath her socks in the dresser, not bothering to close the drawer, and run down the hallway to the main stairs. Ahead of me as I turn the corner, the dark smudge on the carpet changes as I get closer, but I try not to look at it. At *her*, with the blood darkening everything around her, until I'm close enough to actually help.

The pounding in my ears is so loud, like someone's cranked that dance beat higher and higher until my head is ready to burst.

When I get to her, I can't believe it. She's moving, a little. Her hands are still warm as I move them from her throat with one hand and then jab the pen in her leg with the other, like Margot showed me one time when I asked her to.

I wait a second. Two. Three.

I'm sweating all over my body and I think I might die while I'm waiting to fix this awful mistake of mine.

And then Margot shudders and her shoulders heave. I squeeze her hand, hard and firm because I want to let her know she's not alone. I'm here and I'm not going anywhere.

She inhales a rasping breath like a death rattle, but in reverse. Margot sits up suddenly, winces, and then grabs at her side. I watch her take another breath, and another.

"You're going to be okay," I tell her. Her eyes aren't focused yet, but I keep talking to her because that's what I think I'm supposed to do. "Everything's okay."

We sit there a few moments, Margot coming back to life and me marveling at the wonder of science and how it can correct for so many human mistakes.

"What happened?" Margot's breaths are coming steady, so I feel like it's okay to ask her this. I picture the jar of peanut butter my classmates stuffed into my bag. Mom did something with it. "Did somebody give you something?"

Margot blinks and tries to focus them on me, but it's clearly a struggle for her.

"Darren," she says finally, her voice rough and scratchy.

"What do you mean? What about Darren?"

"He's here."

I reflexively reach up and touch the tender spot on my head, where a bump has risen like a hard shell of an egg over the last few hours.

"Daphne," I whisper, and then shout. "We need to find my sister!"

I start to pull Margot up, but she's so heavy and her legs wobble underneath her.

"It's too late," a voice says behind me. A voice I haven't heard for weeks. I don't need to turn around, but I do anyway. I shift so I can look at Darren, pale and thin like a ghost. "You can't help her now."

43

MARK

I'm getting pretty good at playing dead. What I have to do is figure out if I'm good at being alive still. Darren was just here, shooting Brenna full of what I'm assuming is a sedative and then catching a glimpse of something or someone through the window before rushing out.

I sit up in bed, my mind ready for action. I'm weak from not eating much these last few days, but luckily Tobias had snuck me a storehouse of protein bars and granola a few weeks ago, when this lockdown started, and I've been able to live off those for the last few days instead of the food that people brought to me.

I'd suspected for a while that I was being poisoned, but I haven't had the energy or the mental focus to prove it up until I saw my boy, my Felix, staring at his mother the day Margot fell off the horse. He looked so scared. Like he was certain his mother and I couldn't protect him. I told him that day that somebody was coming because I wanted him to be on his guard, but as the drugs wore off and the more my mind cleared I knew I needed to do something. Felix is a survivor, but he's not a fighter. I couldn't leave my children with their mother any longer.

So I stopped eating the food they brought me. Things were getting a little lax anyway, as food supplies dwindled and Brenna became more and more preoccupied with what the lockdown meant for everyone at Granfield. She'd still come in and work from my rooms often enough, but if I'd pretend to be too sleepy to eat she wouldn't push it. Or I'd take a few sips of broth or tea and then have it dribble down my chin, because everyone was coming to expect me to not have much control of my body. My speech was slurring more and more, and even the people closest to me couldn't understand much of what I was saying.

At first, that was exactly how I thought I was going to live the rest of my life. But then Felix's face that day trickled through my fog of pills and self-pity and I knew that I couldn't give up on myself, because that would mean giving up on them—my kids. I wasn't going to accept this lot in life, not without a fight. The doctors we went to see—oh, so many doctors Brenna dragged me to—could never diagnose what was wrong.

But cutting out the food wasn't enough. In the dark hours the next day, I thought about how else someone might be able to hurt me, and then it came: the IVs Margot was told to pump into me each morning. They were supposed to hydrate, and replenish certain essential minerals and fluids. That could do it. And then there are the pills. Pills in the morning and the evening. One big fat pill in the afternoon. On cloudy or rainy days, the only way I could tell how many hours had passed was by the types of pills I was given by Margot. Or Brenna.

Sometimes, even, by Felix or Daphne. Because they'd want to help, I heard them say.

So, I learned to detach my IV and to empty it into my bedpan or into the bathroom, if I could get out of bed without anyone noticing. I also mouthed the pills they gave me. I'd push them underneath my mattress, usually, after I was left alone again. It was easier to do this with Margot gone. She was the one who liked to sit with me and talk for a while. That would have been hard, if I had to keep the pills in my mouth while she told me about her life.

Turns out, after several days of avoiding all the "care" people were giving me, I'm feeling much better. Apparently the treatment was worse than the cure. Not that I'm going to let anyone know I'm feeling back to normal yet.

Brenna and I really loved each other, at first. Or maybe I should say that I really loved her. I can't speak for my wife. Never could. She was a riddle I was certain I could figure out, if I had enough time. Beautiful and calculating and so damn magnetic. I felt like the luckiest man alive when she agreed to marry me.

A small snore escapes from Brenna's mouth, and I decide it's time. I move off the bed, my legs wobbly at first but gaining strength as I move my body more and more, loosening the stiffness that's crept into my bones these last months. I don't know what the poison is that's been slowly eating away at me, but I know Darren stored a lot of chemicals in the greenhouse for the plants and lawn. Any one of those in small enough doses could probably do this damage.

All my clothes are in the bedroom I used to share with Brenna. The only things I have here are hospital scrub tops and pants, loose and thin enough to be easily moved on and off of me when Margot or Brenna would have to change me.

Oh, Margot. Why did she have to come to this house? She doesn't deserve any of this.

I slip on a new shirt and pants, working as quietly as I can and keeping one eye on Brenna at all times. I know I'm not the only one who can pretend to be asleep.

We had a lot of success in our early careers. We were the golden couple, both of us running top-notch power tech companies with fantastic buy-in. Brenna's went public first, with video chat quickly becoming the most influential platform in the world of online companies. The kids came next, and I was so incredibly happy every day with my amazing family, Brenna and I poring over renovation plans by the fire at night with a glass of wine, and Felix and Daphne being both healthy and curious. I loved being a dad. I still do, although I haven't had much of a chance to be a dad to either of them for a while.

Because someone in this house decided to poison me.

And not just my body, but my mind. I never wanted to hurt myself, until I was forced into this hospital bed.

I lunge over to the bathroom, my legs shifting between Charlie-horse stiffness and a looseness that feels foreign, like my muscles can't remember how to work. I turn on the sink and greedily drink several handfuls of water. The liquid seems to immediately rush into my head, like a dam lifting, and my thoughts crystallize into pristine targets.

I have a plan. I know what I need to do.

When I come back out into my room from the bathroom, I notice first thing that Brenna has moved. The smallest bit, so she's slumped over further than I remembered.

I don't have a key card, which means I can't even get out of my *own* medical wing of my *own house*. Thankfully Tobias has been willing to help me move in and out, otherwise I would have been housebound for the last nine months.

I'll have to search her for her key card. I've already scanned the counters and the top of the cabinets and it's not lying anywhere for me to easily grab.

When I go over to Brenna, gingerly bending down to her on the floor, a sudden wooziness overpowers me. I'll have to be careful, I remind myself. I need to stay strong. Don't be stupid. Take it slow and steady.

Brenna's wearing jeans today, not her usual put-together office outfit she's worn for most of our days in quarantine. I know she's been running her business from home, video chatting for hours at a time. I guess video chat is more necessary than ever, when no one can get out to see each other.

She must be making a fortune.

Or, we are, I suppose. Which is exactly the point. It won't be enough for the two of us.

I study my wife's face, and she seems totally out of it. Her breathing is heavy and regular. I lift her arm, and it drops, making a soft thud as it lands on her thigh.

It's now or never. I reach into her pockets and feel for the key card. Her right pocket is empty, and her left is bunched up. I'll have to turn her over slightly in order to get to it.

I'm anxiously aware of the time slipping by since Darren left. I need to go. Now.

I move my sedated wife's body over to the side so that I can reach into her pocket and hopefully get myself out of here, locking her inside behind me. Her arms dangle across me as I shift her over my shoulder.

And that's when I feel it. Her nails, digging hard and fast into my back.

44

MARGOT

"What do you mean, it's too late?" Felix says, and the words jumble inside my mind like clothes in a dryer.

Darren says something, but I can't hear it over the whooshing inside my ears.

Darren, who was dead.

"Why are you here?" I ask, interrupting whatever they're saying. My mouth must not be working quite right because they both look at me strangely, and then Darren slowly moves to stand up from where he'd been crouching beside me.

"You needed my help," he says. "I saw you through the window. But, luckily, someone was here before me."

Felix flinches.

I turn to the dark-haired boy. "Thank you. Thank you for saving me."

I don't ask him about the EpiPen or how he knew where to find it. None of that seems to matter.

Felix's dark eyes stare back at me, and there's so much pain in them in that moment that I have to look away. I start to get up, and Darren reaches out a hand to steady me as I stand.

Felix and I talk at the same time.

"Why are you here?" I repeat to Darren.

"What happened?" Felix asks me.

No one speaks for a few breaths. The three of us move down the hallway and towards the stairs that will lead us outside. It's unspoken, but I think we're all instinctively trying to get out of this house.

And then I remember, as if through a cloud of fog.

The coffee cup and the bitter taste mixed with a slight sweetness as I took a few sips. And then my throat closing in on itself, as if I didn't deserve to breathe after being so easily tricked.

Darren said it's too late.

"Daphne. Where's Daphne?" The panic I'd held at bay these last several minutes, from an anaphylactic episode and the rising of Darren from the dead, decides to attack me now. My voice strains at the ends of each word, like a bow on a violin pulled too tight.

My mother used to play the violin. The memory comes to me, unwanted but still as crisp and clear as what I see in front of me: the hunter-green walls, the silk curtains hung framing each of the tall, spotless windows in a cascade of ruched fabric, the long hallway ahead of us. Darren and Felix walk slowly, and my heart opens a little from all this trauma for their kindness in guiding my broken body and recovering lungs out of this godforsaken house.

I can't see Darren's face, but I feel the tension pull through his arm as he holds on to me and guides me along.

"I saw her through the window."

"You saw a lot of people through the window, didn't you?" Felix says. He doesn't sound scared anymore. He sounds like the almost-teenager that he is, spritely and full of sarcasm.

Darren ignores him.

SARAH K. STEPHENS

"She's lying outside, in the soft patch of grass by the back field. It didn't look like she was sleeping."

Without a word, just a quick flick of his face towards me and a look that was half apology and half terror, Felix lets go of me and takes off running.

I'm trying to make sense of what Darren's said. And what Daphne did, or tried to do, to me.

I never should have come to this house. I never should have come to look for Mark.

"We need to go to her!" I tell Darren as he grips my arm tighter and we continue to make our way towards the outside. A few feet more and I'll be able to breathe in some fresh air and clear out what this house is doing to me, and doing to the people around me.

"We're going. We're almost there," he reassures me.

And we are. A few seconds more, and we're outside in the bright sunshine. A soft breeze blows against our backs, ricocheting off the house.

My head feels almost instantly clearer, being outside of those walls.

We keep moving, no time to waste. I try to listen for sounds of Felix, or of Daphne or anyone else. I try not to think about Brenna, and where she is and how she didn't come to save me. She didn't know that I was in trouble, I tell myself. She wouldn't purposefully try to hurt me.

But could Daphne really make coffee on her own? A few weeks ago, right before all this started, Brenna and I were in the kitchen. I kissed her neck as she sipped from the coffee she'd made. I poured myself a cup.

And then Daphne came in, unannounced, to tell us that she had arrived for the day.

Did she see us together? Did she know I was in love with her mother?

Even if she did, there's no way she could know about why I'm really here at Granfield. Nobody knows that, except for me.

So many things are happening all at once.

We turn a corner, and there she is. Lying like a beautiful doll in the grass, her golden curls kissed by the sun and her cheeks rosy from the heat. Felix crouches over her, looking lost. He's holding her hand in his.

Darren lets go of me and takes off running towards the two of them. "I told you it was too late!" he yells.

Felix blinks, and it seems like he squeezes his sister's hand tighter. "She's still breathing," Felix tells me.

Darren calls out something indistinguishable. He reaches them as I continue to try to stumble closer. I can't quite make it as the pain shoots up my chest and down from my head. There's blood crusted on my cheeks.

I shouldn't be out here, I realize. I'm injured really badly.

But Daphne? What's happened to her?

Darren looks up from Daphne's small body and sees me crumpled on the gravel path.

"Just stay there," he tells me. "There's nothing you can do."

"Felix! Come help me," I order him with as much insistence as I can wrangle into my voice. I'm the only one who can help Daphne. I need to see her pupils. Listen to her breathing. I need to figure out what's happened to her.

My training kicks in, and above the hum of the pain and the delirium from the epinephrine I take charge.

I'll figure out later why Darren is here. What he's been doing these last several weeks when we all thought he was dead. Right now, I need to save this little girl.

"Get me over to her, now!" I shout.

Felix grabs me and hauls me towards Daphne, grunting a bit as he tries to stabilize my body against his. Even though he's been growing, I'm still at least a foot taller than him.

When I'm finally sitting by Daphne, I pull at her eyelids and see that her pupils are widely dilated. I listen to her chest, and her breathing is slow and shallow.

She looks drugged. She looks like she's dying.

I don't have time to figure out if she did this to herself, after she decided to hurt me. Or if someone did this to her.

I bark out orders to Felix and Darren. There's no time to lose.

And maybe just enough time to save her.

45

BRENNA

If someone were to look at us from a distance, they'd think we were lovers. And I guess we are. Were.

My husband flinches as I dig my hands into the pressure points on his back. Darren might be good with plants, but he has no clue how to actually dose a person. I got a little sleepy there for a minute, but now I'm wide awake and ready to finish this. No middlemen this time.

My husband, my family, and me.

Mark is stronger than I thought he'd be, after feeding him small doses of rat poison for so many months. Some days I'd put it into his soup, or his coffee—back when he was drinking coffee. I figured out a way to inject it into his IVs without noticeably puncturing the bags. I'd switch up the ways I gave it to him, in order to keep it less noticeable to Mark and everyone else around him. It was important that it was just enough to weaken him, and make him malinger. I didn't want to kill him. Not that way.

I stand up and Mark follows suit. He makes a grab for my waist and I stumble over him as we both topple to the ground, like two wrestlers in a match. I can't let him leave this room.

"I know what you've been doing," he whispers into my right ear. Whether he whispers because he can't speak any louder, or because he wants me to have to strain to hear him, I'm not sure.

When the plan with the hired men went all wrong, and Tobias and Darren ended up saving Mark and killing them in the process, I had to—as we say in the tech biz—pivot. I'd dosed Mark that night with some weed killer I'd snatched from the greenhouse, to make sure he was feeling sick and too weak to really fight back when they came. After the police arrived and the bodies were carted away, I sat on the staircase in my robe, shaking from nerves and disappointment, and trying to think of my next way out of all of this.

"I know your company's failing." My blood turns to ice as Mark says the words, louder and clearer than anything I've heard him say for a long time.

I jab my free hand into his kidney and he yelps, and then counters by pulling my arms behind my back. I flail with my legs, trying to kick him with enough force to loosen his grip on me, but I can't get enough purchase on the ground or my husband's body to make any real impact.

I'm pinned, my arms pulled back and Mark steadily breathing behind me. I think through what I can do to get free. Eyes, solar plexus, groin, instep. Waves of memories from a long-ago self-defense class I took when I was trying on having female friends come back to me, reminding me of the weakest places in a man.

Their minds are even weaker still. I knew I had Mark from the moment I met him, even though he was dating that Teresa back then. It was more than a little convenient that she died in a car crash, just as Mark was starting to get tired of her. He's the type of man who would feel guilty for the rest of his life if he left one woman for another. With Teresa gone, he didn't have to feel guilty.

He just had to grieve.

"I don't know what you're talking about." I say it into the air, staring out the window from beside Mark's bed. There are dark smudges moving on the ground in the distance. I think about Daphne, and the way my body revolted when I gave her the juice I'd been saving in the back of the cupboard. The one I was able to dose with the same chemicals I've been using for months to eat away at Mark, only this time I made the dose heavier.

I don't want my children to see any of this. They deserve to think of their lives as beautiful, with loving parents and a world that wants them. And if I can't give them that anymore, then it's time to end it.

I didn't have a chance to find Felix because I was interrupted by Darren, who somehow survived—Tobias has a lot to answer for. I should have realized he was weak. I should have stayed there, with Tobias, and seen it through to the end. When Darren showed up, sick with the flu, it was the perfect opportunity to kick off what I'd been planning for months, as soon as those first headlines of the virus hit. I'd already laid the groundwork online, and set up the filters on the internet portals. Just one click, and I could put everything in motion.

Mark's voice comes back from behind me. "Your company, the video chat, is having some legal issues. You didn't ensure the right protections to avoid being liable for what people do on your app, did you? Always pushing ahead to the next greatest thing, right, Brenna? Never stopping to check on the rules or the regulations."

The fury I've kept under control for these weeks, for months really, burns hot and white in the center of my belly. No one gets to talk about my work like this, not even my husband.

"We didn't do anything wrong!"

"Except you did, and now your company's going to run itself

into the ground paying all the fines you've been charged with. Which is why you need *my* money. *My* business."

"We share everything," I say through gritted teeth.

"You know that's not true." Mark pulls at my arms and I release some of the tension in my shoulders, relaxing into his hold just slightly. I want him to think I'm getting tired. Weak.

He goes on. "With me incapacitated for the last year or so, you've been able to siphon money into your company from mine, without me ever knowing. Or that's what you thought. Thank goodness you have a habit of leaving your laptop in here. You still have terrible passwords—our wedding anniversary?"

"What's wrong with one spouse helping another?" I slump my shoulders. I ease into it.

Mark doesn't say anything for a long while. We stay there, my arms wrapped behind me and held against his still-broad chest, and again I think about how from the outside it looks like we're embracing each other rather than permanently erasing the connections we once had.

"I would have done anything for you," Mark finally says. He whispers it, and this time I'm certain he chooses to say it quietly, a secret between the two of us.

Although a small part of me, buried deep inside and covered with slick layers of resentment and disappointment, still loves my husband, I can't let that piece of me smother the rest of who I am.

"No," I tell him, heavy with longing. "But you will."

And that's when I buck my head back so it catches Mark's nose.

His face instantly bursts into a waterfall of blood. Felix told me once, head bent over that damn outmoded biology textbook of his, that there are more blood vessels in the nose than anywhere else on the rest of the body. Mark reflexively lets go and reaches up to staunch the bleeding.

I run to the door, ready to get the hell out of there, but when I get to the keypad and check my pockets to retrieve the key card, it's not there.

I scramble around, becoming more and more frantic with each passing second.

"I have it," Mark tells me. I've never heard his voice sound so hollow.

I turn and see one hand holding up the tail of his shirt to his nose. In the other is the key card he managed to slip from my pocket while I was thinking about us looking like two people who loved each other.

46

FELIX

Daphne is going to be okay. That's what Margot keeps saying, like a music track clicked on to repeat.

Darren still looks worried though, and Daphne's eyes aren't normal. They look like a werewolf version of her. But Margot has more confidence than the rest of us, and the knots in my chest want to believe what she's saying.

"We need to get inside somewhere," Darren says quietly. "We need to get out of sight."

He picks up Daphne's body and carries her to the stables. Margot and I sit there like two statues and watch him go for a few moments, until my arms and legs move almost like they're part of some robot version of myself and, finally, we follow Darren and my sister.

"I don't think we should be in here," Margot says as we cross the threshold from the brightness of the day into the damp warm air of the horses' home.

"We can't stay outside where she can see us." Darren twists his head round, looking for a place to put Daphne down. He finally stops on a chest where I know Tobias keeps extra saddles and old bridles. It's long and wooden, with a horse blanket thrown over the top.

Darren lays my sister down, and she lets out a small "uff", even though I can tell from where I'm standing that Darren is being really gentle.

"Who do you mean?" Margot asks. "Brenna? Brenna would never hurt her children. She'd never hurt anyone."

Margot wraps her arms around her shoulders as she says it, like she's cold, although the air in the stable is humid and musty. I pull at the neck of my T-shirt and stretch it out a little, but it snaps back into place as soon as I let go. My hands feel like I've just washed them, they're so clammy.

Darren casts a sideways glance at Margot.

They look at each other for a moment, and I know what they're thinking. That night Daphne and I were forced to stay in the panic room, when Tobias carried Daphne from the stables and Mom came to check on us a few times, but we spent the entire evening into the next day waiting and waiting. Mom came on the video monitor one time, late into the night, and she looked so scared.

No, I correct myself even as I think it.

Not scared. She looked mad. Not the kind of mad where I forgot to make my bed in the morning or Greta forgot to buy organic cereal. Mad, like crazy.

Darren was supposed to be dead, because my mom said so.

"She was trying to keep us all safe. You were sick, really sick, and the recovery rate for the virus is so low, especially for children. She couldn't let you infect them," Margot says. "How are you even alive?"

One of the horses, Jasmine or Julie or one of the others, gives a long nicker, like they're in on some sort of joke.

And then, from the shadows, Tobias appears, holding a shovel in his hands with the shovel head poised at his shoulder.

"He's alive because of me," Tobias tells us. "Because I couldn't kill him, the way Brenna wanted me to."

Darren won't look at Tobias, but Margot can't seem to look away from him. Him and that shovel.

I want to scream. And this time, I do.

"Who cares? What's happening to Daphne? What happened to her?" I shout as loud as my lungs will let me, and my voice turns screechy at the end of it all.

The three adults turn and stare at me for a beat, and then they whirl into action. Margot rushes over to Daphne's side, wincing as she moves, and takes her pulse and whispers things to her. My sister's lips move, slowly but still moving all the same. From where I'm standing, I can't see her eyes and whether they're still large like an animal's, but I watch her chest going up and down as Margot counts out loud and Daphne breathes with the rhythm.

At the same time, Darren moves away from my sister. He and Tobias square off across the middle aisle of the stables. Tobias still has the shovel hoisted up, and his knuckles turn white as he grips it harder.

The horses don't like any of this. Noise fills the stable, with the horses nickering and whinnying. Jasmine and Julie are up front closest to us and they paw the ground with their hooves. The sound of dirt being scratched by huge animals drowns out the voices of the grown-ups and soon it's all I can hear in my ears.

That, and the sound of my beating heart, still hoping my mother will come and save us.

47

DARREN

"We don't have time for this," I tell Tobias. He's making me nervous with that shovel gripped so tight in his hands.

"I know that," he replies, but his grip doesn't loosen. He turns his eyes over to the left, where Daphne's sitting up a little as Margot supports her back with her hand. The tension at Margot's temples and mouth tell me how much she's hurting, but she keeps tending to the little girl. Guilt burns deep inside my chest.

"What happened to Daphne?" Tobias goes on.

The words run out of my mouth like a swarm of angry insects, looking to bite. "Her mother poisoned her."

Confusion cuts across Tobias' face, followed by something else. His grip on the shovel loosens a little.

I can see him working through it in his head.

How he left me in my apartment, thinking that it would be easier on his conscience if he let me die *naturally*, burning with fever and choking on my own phlegm. He'd read, like I had for the last several days leading up to the lockdown, that the virus works rapidly and that I'd be dead in a few more hours.

All he'd have to do was quarantine my apartment, which they'd want to do anyway, and then clear out my body later when it was safe to do so.

No killing on his conscience, and Brenna would never know the difference.

But I survived. I passed out soon after he left me, and when I woke up the next morning I was already feeling better. My fever had broken and my breathing was easier. I was weak, but I was recovering.

When I looked out the window of my apartment by the bed, I saw the bonfire smoldering. Tobias had been clever. He'd tossed in some of my clothes at the edge, so they'd char a little but still be visible. Brenna would believe that the rest of me had been eaten by the fire.

She was there, staring at the flames and covering her face with the sleeve of her sweatshirt to keep the smoke out. Looking at her face, that's when I knew we were over, if there ever even was a we. Because Brenna stared at the fire, and she smiled.

Not a little smile, like she was thinking of something small and beautiful to help her deal with the tragedy surrounding us. Not like she was recalling a memory she held close to her and went to in times of awfulness, like I hold on to the memories of my little girl—and which I've had to use to help me a lot these last two weeks.

No, she was smiling like she'd just finished a marathon and she had the numbers called out on TV for the lottery and been told by the most wonderful person that she was the one for them.

She was smiling like a winner.

"Why didn't you come back to the house?" Tobias asks me, but he knows as soon as he says it that it's a stupid question. Of course I didn't come back. The woman in charge had told him to kill me in order to supposedly keep her family safe. She wasn't going to stand for me sauntering up, supposedly cured and ready to help again.

Of course, Tobias doesn't know the other reason Brenna wanted me dead.

Margot murmurs in the background. Felix moves a little to my right, and I realize I'd almost forgotten he was there. It must be hard, being so easily ignored by people.

And maybe sometimes an advantage too, I think.

"Did you set the greenhouse on fire?" Felix asks, and I flinch at the sound of his voice. He's so pale, with dark rings under his eyes. He reaches up and rubs his head at the back.

"Does your head hurt?" I tried to be as gentle as I could. Maybe if I'd been harder, he would still be safely up in his room.

"Answer the question," Tobias chimes in.

"No, I didn't." I loved those plants. I love the idea of helping life grow. I'd never burn them down.

"What about the fox?" Tobias asks next. "What have you been living on?"

"What fox?" I have no idea what he's talking about, and Margot's face tells me she's just as clueless. "I had food in my cupboard. All of you were avoiding my apartment, so I was able to get in and out pretty easily when I needed something. That is, until this one showed up, wanting my key card." I nod towards Felix, and the poor boy promptly turns a bright red.

"I didn't know you had one. It was a hunch," he explains.

Tobias shakes his head. "What do you mean?"

Felix squares his shoulders towards me. "You hit me, didn't you? You're the one who knocked me down and then put me in my room?"

I don't say a word. I focus on my breathing, keeping it steady and strong.

Behind me, Daphne whispers something to Margot.

Tobias repeats, "What do you mean?"

Felix points his finger at me, and a slight tremble appears at the tip of his index finger. "He knocked me unconscious, just before Margot had her attack. And before Daphne ended up outside, almost dead too."

"I didn't do anything, except try to keep you safe," I tell Felix. I tell all of them.

Tobias grips the shovel tighter. I sense Margot standing up behind me.

"Daphne says Darren did it. That she saw him set the greenhouse on fire. And that he's the one who poisoned her," Margot tells our group.

Fury spreads across Tobias' face and blood pounds in my ears.

I explain. "Brenna did it. She's not who she seems to be."

But before I can continue, Jasmine's heavy head whips up and down, slamming into the crown of my head, and I crumple to the ground.

"Good girl," I hear Tobias say. "Good girl."

48

MARK

Brenna stares back at me with a mixture of outrage and dread.

"Give it to me," she demands, as though I'm one of the kids. Or one of her employees. Like she expects me to submit to her, even though I know she'll kill me the instant she has the chance.

My body throbs all over, but there's an energy to it that seems to propel me forward. My weakness from what my wife's done to me these last few months has transformed into something else. I picture Daphne and Felix's faces, and know that I have to do it now.

I reach for the gun Darren tucked between the mattresses of my bed, I'm assuming to store for safekeeping until he came back for it. I pull the gun out and aim it at my wife.

"It's over," I tell her. A wave of sadness, sudden and disorienting, rips through me like a current through the ocean, and then it's gone. I don't have time to grieve the loss of my marriage, or the betrayal of someone who I promised to love forever. I can't think about how Brenna has decided to ruin me, body and soul, to save her company.

For money and prestige.

Instead, I have to focus on pointing this weapon that we chose together at her as precisely as possible, and what I'm going to do next if she refuses to follow my orders. Or, even more importantly, what I'm going to do if she listens.

Brenna puts her hands up, as if in surrender.

She still looks as though she could cut me apart with her eyes, but she steps away from the door. It doesn't pass without my notice that, by stepping further from the door, she's also moved closer to me.

"I know," she tells me. She takes another step away from the exit.

"Don't come any closer." I hold the gun and click back the hammer.

"Are you really going to shoot me?" Brenna asks. "I'm the mother of your children. Your wife. You love me. And think about what people will say. What they'll think. You'll go to prison, and then our children will be parentless. You'll ruin everything."

"Yes, I'm going to shoot you." But my words come out hollow and unmoored. I've always been a terrible liar. It's Brenna who had the gift for "wordplay", as she called it, which I can see now was really just the ability to manipulate others.

"I don't think you are."

Brenna moves towards me, so close that I can see the scar on her forehead from when she was a little girl. The fire was caused by faulty electrical wiring, they found out later. She had to go live with her grandmother, after her parents' funerals. She had nothing left, because all her toys and clothes and photos from when she was little burned up in the fire.

"It made me who I am today", she'd told me as we lay under the covers in my dorm room, holding tight and trying to ease each other from our own private griefs. I'd lost Teresa just a few weeks before. Getting that phone call in the middle of the night telling me that my girlfriend had died in a car accident was the first time the world showed me that it was anything other than a wonderful place. I was almost a grown man.

For Brenna, she knew that truth even before she could tie her own shoelaces.

We each have our moments of reckoning, I suppose. Mine should have been losing Teresa, I realize now. But it wasn't. I still trusted in the goodness of people. In the rightness of the world. Teresa's death was an accident, it wasn't the status quo of life.

But now, pointing a gun at my wife of fifteen years and having to decide if I'll make my children motherless, or let them lose their father, it's never been clearer to me that the world is a terrible violent place.

"Do it," Brenna taunts me.

And so I do.

49

MARGOT

I pull back Darren's eyelids and his pupils respond to the light on my phone. His breathing is steady and deep enough. He has a welt forming on the side of his head, but other than that he seems to be dozing in a worriless sleep.

I turn my gaze to Daphne, who is looking less and less pale by the minute, but who still holds her arms over herself like a wild animal has cornered her. We've tied Darren's hands and feet together and pulled him into an unused stall towards the back of the stable, but none of that has changed the way Daphne holds herself.

Felix rubs at the back of his neck.

Tobias doesn't have any visible wounds, but as soon as we finished moving Darren into the stall he went back and grabbed the shovel, its head poised high above his shoulder.

My ribs and head ache. My throat burns.

So many of us here at Granfield are damaged, I think.

"We need to find Mom and Dad," Felix says.

I see Daphne shake her head, slightly.

"Tobias can stay with Darren," I reason. "I'll go with Felix back to the house."

"No!" Daphne shouts. "No, we have to stay together."

"We need to make sure Mom and Dad are safe," Felix says to his sister. "No one has seen them in a long time. And we don't know what Darren might have done to them."

A shudder flashes up my spine. I think of the altar under the tree that Brenna told me about. The bloody doll. Why would Darren do that?

My hands shake as I bring them to my face and run them through my hair, trying to think. It was Daphne who gave me the coffee, she's the one who wanted me to have an allergic reaction.

Or was it Brenna?

There's no way Darren could have done that, could he? But had Darren been inside the house? And why was Daphne looking so normal already. She hasn't vomited or anything, and her pupils and breathing are back to normal. It's almost like she was faking.

What did Darren really do to her, if anything?

"Daphne," I snap, harsher than I mean to be. "Who helped you make the coffee for me?"

Daphne stares at her feet. "No one."

Felix interrupts. "We need to go, now! We need to find Mom!"

"Why did you do it?" I lean closer to her little cherub face. "Why did you try to hurt me?"

"That's enough," Tobias says and steps between us. "She's traumatized, can't you see that?" He turns to me. "And you're badgering her about some sort of nonsense."

"I almost died!" I want to scream at how absurd it feels to have to justify my anger at almost dying less than two hours ago. "If it weren't for Felix, and Darren too," I add, "I would be dead. I would have asphyxiated from an allergic reaction, and died."

Tobias backs off. "I didn't know. Are you okay?"

I ignore him and look at Daphne, but she avoids my gaze.

"Why, Daphne?"

The horses don't like any of this.

"What's going on?" Felix asks his little sister, raising his voice again. "What did you do?"

The horses don't like any of this.

Daphne twists her hands in her lap.

"I saw her kissing Mom." Her words have no weight. They are as light as air, coming from her small child voice, and yet it's like a bomb exploded in the room and all the oxygen has been sucked out from the aftershock.

"What?" Felix says. It's like a live electrical wire is connected to his feet, but it hasn't grounded itself yet. He's all energy, coiled and ready to leap, but without an endpoint.

I can't believe I was so stupid. My sisters, my family—they would be so ashamed.

Tobias won't look at me. Daphne stares ahead, a small curve turning up the corner of her mouth. "I saw her kissing our mother," she repeats.

She goes on. "It's not right. Mommy and Daddy love each other. But if Mommy kisses Margot, then she and Daddy won't be together anymore and we'll have to go somewhere else and we won't be able to see each other or stay at our same school or with our friends or live in the same house. That's what happened to Tommy Winger at school, and now everyone hates him and he kind of smells and he's always sad."

"So you decided to *kill* Margot!" Felix springs into action, flailing his arms and kicking out his legs. He grips his sister by the shoulders and shakes her violently for a few seconds, until Tobias and I pry him off.

Daphne is terrified and bunches herself into a ball on the ground.

"You're stupid, so stupid!" Felix shouts at his sister.

"That's enough." Tobias stands in the middle of the stables. "We need to get out of here. We need to find Brenna and Mark."

He turns to me. "Are you okay?"

I nod.

"All four of us will go. Darren is fine where he is. I've got him tied tight to the post. We'll come back and check on him once we find your mom and dad."

Tobias walks out of the stable doors, and the three of us follow silently behind him.

I stay towards the back, not willing to give anyone the advantage over me again.

As we walk to the big house, I see Felix hesitate—reaching out, and then back, and then out again—to offer Daphne his hand. After a moment's pause she takes it. The two of them, brother and sister, hold on to each other as they walk to the main house, in search of their parents.

50

BRENNA

Mark shoots the gun pointed straight at my chest. He pauses a second, as though he can't believe what's happened.

But the gun was never loaded. I'm not stupid enough to keep a firearm around two young children with bullets loaded in it. It was more the threat of it—the look of it—that I needed. Plus, despite what you see on all those TV shows, it's also not the best idea to have a loaded gun nestled into the crook of your back, even if the safety is on. When I found Darren in my office, I wasn't scared that he took the gun. I was scared of what he'd do to me when he realized it wasn't loaded.

Mark and I come at each other like two wild animals, all fangs and claws and crazed sounds.

He tries to wrap his arms around me in a bear hug, but I jam my fingers in his mouth first. He bites down hard, but not hard enough. I push back further, gripping at the soft flesh of his tongue, and pull. Mark lets go of me and I take my hand out, just as quickly, and jab it into his windpipe.

I took self-defense with Mark's girlfriend back in college. That's how she and I became friends. Or what she thought was friends. That's how I managed to get her drunk one night and so down on herself that she drove out into the farmland surrounding the edges of campus. I told her how I'd overheard Mark telling some of his friends that she was just a way station for him. That he was going to break up with her when someone better came along. I told her he'd said he didn't think she was pretty, or smart or interesting, but that she was easy to get into bed. The real clincher though, was when I told her that he said he pictured someone else while they were having sex.

I didn't need to tell her that he was picturing me. She already knew. Everybody did.

Mark wanted to be with me, but he couldn't deal with the guilt of breaking up with Teresa, especially with her mother's suicide a few years earlier and all of her sisters needing her. It made it that much easier to explain her self-destructive behavior though, after the accident. The apple doesn't fall far from the tree, and all that.

I throw myself at Mark. He's six inches taller than me, but nine months of bed rest have made him weak. I only need to get my hands around his neck in the right way. Don't think about it, Brenna. Get it done.

He squirms under the pressure of my hands, but I'm able to lean against him just so, using the pressure points I learned about in that damn class with Teresa, and hold firm. He grabs at my arms and holds tight to me for a few more seconds, but his body is too weakened from what I've done to him these past several months to be a real fighter.

When Mark slumps to the ground, unconscious, I wait a few more seconds before ripping the sheets off the bed and coiling them into a tight rope that stretches across the room. I don't have much time, but I'm making good progress when I hear voices calling from deep inside the house.

I stop and listen for a second. I don't hear the strong

accented English, or another language I don't recognize. Instead, I hear the voices of my children—*both* of them—high and strained, calling out to me and to their father.

I have to keep moving. I have to get this done.

I grab the gun, run to the safe, and load the bullets. Just in case.

Nothing is going the way it's supposed to.

Trying to count back from when I caught Darren on the laptop in the library, I figure I have maybe thirty more minutes before they arrive, guns drawn and ready for action. It was so stupid to involve Darren, when I arranged that first group of men to come and try to kidnap my husband. I thought Darren would stick to the plan, collect the money I'd agreed to pay him, and then move on.

Instead, he decided to be the big hero, and then to stay on at Granfield. Taunting me with the information he had over me. Luckily he didn't figure out that Mark's illness was something I was controlling. He really thought Mark was dying, and I can only assume that's why he didn't turn me in. He wanted me to be there for Mark, in the end.

It goes to show you that kindness is no kindness. All I've ever gotten from this world has been by fighting for it.

Daphne and Felix's faces swim to the surface of my thoughts, but I push them down. I fought for them too, when it comes down to it. I fought to have Mark, and then I fought to keep him.

But sometimes other things get in the way. I made a name for myself, and I can't let all of that slip away. I can always find a new husband. What I can't do is build a new company, from the ground up. My reputation for failure would follow me everywhere I go. Especially as a woman in tech? No one would ever touch me again. I'd be finished.

And I'm not willing to let that happen. There've been too many of us already, gasping for air in the trenches of this fucking boys' club. I'm not going down with them. I'm a trailblazer.

I'm making the world a better place for other women.

As I wrap the sheet around Mark's neck, I recall the knots I read about before wiping the servers clean. Some knots can be tied by the person making the noose. Others are tied by someone else only.

I tie the one that Mark could have done himself.

Before I drag my unconscious husband over to the window, I do a quick search of his pockets and retrieve the key card. I don't have time to stop and think. I can only do.

He deserves this, I tell myself. He shot you. Or he would have, had there been any bullets in the gun. He was ready to murder you.

I ignore the small voice inside my head reminding me that it wouldn't have been murder. It would have been self-defense.

Daphne's voice is closest. "Mommy! Daddy!"

What have I done?

I'm ready and poised at the windowsill. I've secured the sheet to the bed and it's wrapped around Mark's neck with a tight noose. All I have to do is lift him up and over, and then let go.

Just let go.

The doors to the outer room are opening. All the machines in Mark's room are silent without a patient to monitor. I can hear Mark's soft breathing and the whir of the locks loosening, about to let my children in.

It has to be now.

I lift Mark up, propping his torso on the edge of the windowsill and then lifting his legs over. He falls out the window and the sheet snaps tight around his neck. The bed holds steady. I can't look over, but I hear scratching and realize he must not have fallen hard enough to snap his neck. I force the image of Mark's legs flailing from the lack of air in his lungs out of my mind. He's suffocating.

And I'm standing here, looking at my children and my lover and this man I barely know, trying to make them believe that I had nothing to do with any of this.

"Help me," I cry out. "He's dying!"

51

TOBIAS

I grab the sheet and rip it up in big handfuls. It only takes a few seconds, but I've no idea how long Mark has been hanging there.

Margot and I scramble to get it off his neck as Brenna corrals the children in a corner of the room, shielding what they can see with her body.

He's not breathing as we unwind the cloth from his neck, and Margot starts CPR on him in precise and practiced movements. She goes on for a minute, two minutes. Seconds stretch and pass by in long fuzzy gaps. She calls out to me to do certain things, like hold his legs or press down on his shoulders, and I do what I'm told.

But I don't take my eyes off Brenna for a second.

52

MARGOT

This can't be happening. I'm a good nurse. I'm capable and strong, and I can save him.

I keep doing the compressions. I keep breathing into his mouth.

I remember once, in nursing class, learning about a woman who did CPR on her husband for twenty minutes before he had a response. If she'd given up too soon, he'd be dead.

She kept believing in her own ability to save him, and so she did.

Thoughts scurry across my mind, and I can't hold on to any of them except for counting inside my head. And the fact that I never got to tell him about my sister. I never got to thank him for loving her. Or to confront him about the night she died.

He'd been the only thing, besides me and my other sisters, to get Teresa through our mother's death. I remember her calling and telling me about this wonderful guy, smart and handsome and so very kind, who she'd been dating for a few weeks. This was maybe two or three months after Teresa had come home from college for a weekend visit and found our mother in the bathtub, a stream of vomit spread over her chest and her body cold and rigid. She'd finally taken enough pills to actually kill herself this time.

I was already in high school, about to finish up my junior year. Our other sisters were in college or working. Debbie had gotten married right out of high school and was already a mom to a little baby girl.

Teresa wouldn't let me see Mom when I came home from soccer practice. Not like that.

We buried her and moved on with our lives, or at least I thought. It hadn't really come as a surprise to any of us. It felt more like an inevitability and, for me, a piece of relief too, that I didn't have to worry about when it was coming anymore, asking myself when would Mom finally do it.

I stayed with a friend of mine's family for the next year until I graduated. My other sisters kept living their lives, but Teresa struggled. She was thinking about dropping out of school. She couldn't eat, couldn't focus on her studies. She'd come back to our little town every weekend to check on me, supposedly. But I knew she was also searching for something. Some explanation for what happened to our mother.

I already knew. There was no answer. It just was. Our mother was sad. Very sad. And then she tried to die. And then she died. The end.

But then Teresa had met Mark, and her life changed. Until one night, she called and left me a voicemail. I was already asleep, and when I woke up the next morning I listened to her message where she slurred her words as she sobbed into the phone, telling me that she was worthless. That Mark didn't really love her, like our mother didn't love her. That he'd been saying things about her, terrible nasty things.

She was going to confront him. But first, she needed to go for a drive. Get some fresh air and space.

She sounded drunk from the start of the message.

As I finished listening to it there was a knock on the bedroom door, and my friend's dad was outside it with a police officer in a uniform standing next to him.

That's how I found out my big sister had died in a car crash. A drunk driving crash.

She was pegged by everyone as a typical result of a crazy mother and absentee father. And I swore I'd find Mark Stone one day, and I'd make things right again for my sister.

And for me.

So I keep pumping his chest.

I was going to do it when he was so far gone that it wouldn't be surprising or questioned. Give him a dose of medication that was a little too strong for his weakened heart, and he'd drift off into a dreamless sleep.

I didn't want him to suffer. Not really. I only wanted him to pay for his cruelty.

And before I did it, I was going to tell him that I was Teresa's sister. That I knew what he'd done to her. How he'd used her. And that he deserved what was coming to him.

I'd convinced myself that I could do it, even though I'd had so many chances in the past to have him slip away without any suspicion on my part. I mean, he was trying to kill himself on a regular basis. I could have let one of those go too far, tend to him a little too late.

But I couldn't do it.

Which is why I'm pumping his heart for him and breathing his breath for him.

I'm not a killer. Not even for Teresa.

Especially not for Teresa, I realize now.

53

BRENNA

Mark isn't dead.
   Mark is dead.

I don't have time to figure out which is true. Margot keeps hunching over his chest and pressing life back into him, and I'm hugging my children close to me as though I'm a good mother.

"You need to stop," Tobias tells Margot. He puts a steady hand on her shoulder, but she won't stop. "Margot, he's gone."

"Not yet," she tells him in between pulses on Mark's chest.

"He wanted to die," Tobias says, so quietly that I almost can't hear him. He's trying to spare the children from hearing it, which is so absurd to me and at the same time so kind that I want to weep into their pale, frightened faces and tell them that the world isn't all eat or be eaten.

But the moment passes, as they always do. And I'm left with everything I've been planning these last several weeks, months, years in tatters and I need to figure out how I'm going to fix this. There's no time for grief or regret. I need to keep going.

"What's happening?" I call out from across the room. "Mark! Is he going to be okay?"

Felix grips me tighter and Daphne's nails dig into my side.

Tobias holds on to Margot's arms and pulls her away from Mark's body, which is starting to take on a cast to it that is different from the softness of someone who is breathing on their own. The sheet lies in a tangled mass, like a spider's nest, in the corner underneath the window.

Margot shouts and protests, kicking at Tobias and trying to pull herself free with her arms, but he holds firm and she eventually stops and settles into his hold. She turns to me, and our eyes meet for the first time since we've come together in this sick room.

"I tried," she cries out to me. "I tried to save him! I didn't want him to die."

I can't stop myself. Even though my children are clinging to me and my husband is lying dead just twenty feet from me, her words poke something inside my brain that won't settle. I see an opening.

"Why would you have wanted him to die? Why would you even need to defend yourself?"

I move towards Margot, like a magnet's pulling me along into this inevitability, and Felix steps away from me as I walk. A small sob escapes his mouth, which he promptly claps a hand over. I cast a sidelong glance his way. "It's okay, sweetheart," I tell my son. "I'm going to make everything better."

Daphne still has her arms wrapped around me, and when I look down her eyes are huge black disks of terror. Or excitement. Or a little of both.

She's always been my ally, ever since she came into the world, screaming like a banshee and not willing to tolerate anything other than total respect for her specialness. Daphne is absolutely her mother's daughter.

I wasn't going to ask her to help me with the teas and the meals for her father, but she was so curious. Following me around like a little shadow. And with the habits of a magpie.

One day I was in the medical wing with Mark, mixing up his special supplements, as they were, and she appeared out of nowhere. She'd gotten ahold of the extra key card I kept in our safe—how she figured out the combination we used back then I'm still not sure—and come in at her own leisure. She's only seven, but she knew something wasn't right with what I was doing, and so I told her she'd be my helper. I made sure to emphasize that I wasn't asking her brother for help. It was only going to be her and me.

And so she and I worked together, mother and daughter, a perfect team. Until Tobias told me about the fox, sliced open in the stables. In the medical ward, while her father slept, I'd told Daphne about protection. About how to defend herself. We'd practiced those moves, cutting into the air. In case someone ever came, I told her, she would know how to protect herself. But hearing about what she did to that animal—that's when I knew I'd gone too far with her. I hadn't just made her fierce and ready for battle in this world of men. I'd made her a killer, someone who does it just for the sake of dominating someone or something else. I'd made her a liability.

"What are you talking about?" Margot cries out. I watch Tobias' grip on her shift slightly. He's still holding her back, but he changes the position of his hands so he's also almost pushing her out, towards me.

"What did you do?" I say. I'm so close to her that I can see the beads of sweat on her forehead from the pressure she put on Mark's chest to try to resuscitate him. "What have you done?"

"Nothing! I was only trying to help."

"She poisoned me," Daphne says. She's turned her face against my legs, and her chin is pressed into my thigh so tightly that her chin wobbles against the muscles of my leg as she tries to talk. "Margot put something in my juice, and I almost died."

I hit Margot's face. The face that I held so close to mine,

kissing the soft skin of her collarbone. The tender corners of her eyes and mouth. I slap her hard, and a welt appears on her face almost as soon as I connect with her skin.

I haul back, ready to strike again, when I notice Tobias. Something is off. He's pulling Margot back, away from me, and inserting himself in between us.

"Hold on to her," I shout out into the void of the room. "She hurt my daughter. She killed my husband!"

"Stop it," Tobias growls. He looks at Daphne, then at me. "Get away from her."

"You said Darren did it to you." Felix has crept from the corner of the room. He won't turn his eyes to look at me directly, because then he'd have to take in his father's body. I want to wrap my arms around him and promise that everything will be okay, and then have him drift off into a different world where he doesn't have to see any of this. My tender, patient, weak little boy.

"No, I didn't." Daphne shakes her head. "I never said that at all. It was Margot!" Her face looks flushed as she points a tiny finger at our resident nurse.

"Stop lying!" Felix runs over and grabs his sister off of me. He pushes her to the ground, straddling her tiny body. "Stop pretending this is a game! What did you do?" He slaps her across the face, to all of our horror, like I slapped Margot a few moments ago.

Daphne starts to cry. Felix stays on top of her, not turning his body towards the corner with the window. He raises his arm again, and before I can reach out to stop him or Tobias can work his way from Margot over to the two of them, he clenches his fingers into a fist and swings down in an arc towards his sister's face.

54

DAPHNE

I don't think Felix really wants to hurt me. He saw Darren come through the open door, the one Tobias forgot to close when we found Daddy. All the grown-ups were distracted.

I wanted to keep them that way.

I don't want to help Mommy ever again.

She taught me how to lie, and I'm really good at it. Sometimes I lie without even thinking about it, just because I can. Mommy taught me how to hurt other people. But I don't want to do any of that anymore. I want to be a good girl.

Because if I'm a good girl, maybe Daddy will sit up and come back and read me stories about dancing princesses and men who try to figure out where they go at night. That's how I knew to let the juice dribble down my chin. Like the princes who didn't drink the special potion and were able to follow the princesses into their secret dancing hall in the middle of the night.

That's why I pretended like I was really sick outside, because Mommy wanted to hurt me too. She thought I hadn't seen her do it, but I was watching longer than she thought as she got the juice out and the glass. I'm really good at sneaking around, too.

I couldn't let her hurt me.

Felix is pretending like he's going to hit me, so all the grown-ups are looking at us and they won't see Darren getting ready in the corner. I hope he'll forgive me for what I said in the stables, because I think he's the only one who can make Mommy stop.

55
DARREN

Brenna doesn't see me yet.

It's different from how it felt when she came to me, almost a year ago, wanting more than just attention. Wanting help. Right now she doesn't see me because Felix is creating a distraction. But back then, she didn't see me, not really, because I wasn't a person to her. I should have known from the beginning that she didn't think of me as anything other than a tool that she could use and then discard. I wasn't anything beyond the purposes she saw me serving.

I was out in the greenhouse, working on getting the gardens ready for spring—last spring—when she knocked on the metal door and asked me if I'd mind if she watched me work. I didn't, and I said so, and then she took a seat and started saying these things, wild and exciting and dangerous things from my past that we'd never talked about before, even during those times when the corners of her eyes would soften as we lay together afterwards and I'd think "This is was what trust looks like". And then it was her asking me for help. She knew I was on my own, that my daughter had died from that awful disease that no one could do anything about—leukemia —and that my wife and I had split up for good afterwards. I'd gotten mixed up in some messes after that. Drunk driving, some drug selling to make ends meet, and I got to know who the powerful bad people around the area were. My mother was a Russian immigrant, and so I could speak their language pretty well, which helped.

I'm good with my hands, and it seems like all sorts of people need someone like that—rich and poor, good and bad. They all need someone who knows how to make things work. Before I came to Granfield, I was deep inside with some of them, getting their handiwork done and some not-so-handy work too. But I couldn't live with myself anymore, and so I came here.

I won't say my former bosses were happy about it, but they also weren't going to stop me. I told them I just needed some time, and that I'd come back some day. When I said it I didn't think it was true, but then Brenna came around with her pearly teeth and her tailored-to-within-an-inch-of-her life finesse and she told me she needed my help.

Tobias is great with horses, just ask the bruise swelling on the back of my head from where Jasmine's jaw caught me. But he's terrible at knots. It only took me a few seconds to wriggle loose from them once I woke up.

I have the shotgun tucked under my arm, the one Tobias used to hide in the stables until he asked me to hide it in my apartment. The one that brought Brenna's first plan crashing down when he fired it at a few of my friends the night they tried to kidnap Mark. The one Felix almost found when he came snooping, before I distracted him with that whole mess of water and steam in my bathroom.

It's loaded, ready to aim and fire, but I don't want it to come to that. I'm hoping I can be persuasive without having to hurt anyone.

I've done enough of that in my lifetime.

Felix is going to hit Daphne again. I feel sick to my stomach, even though I'm certain they're only fighting in order to give me an opening. I hear Felix's hand connect with Daphne's face again, and the soft snap of his skin against her cheek makes me want to throw up.

"It's over, Brenna." I hoist the gun up on my shoulder, careful to keep everyone in my view. Margot and Tobias don't understand yet what's going on, and I don't have time to explain, because my friends are coming very soon.

I've set things in motion and there's no turning back.

Brenna twists from her children and takes me in, her eyes turning from the terror-filled look she put on for her kids into that nasty coolness I remember glimpsing in the stairwell when Granfield was under attack, and Mark had a gun pointed to his head.

Oh, Mark. I can't bring myself to glance over to him in the corner. He was a good man. He was the kind of man I wanted to be.

He didn't deserve any of this.

"Drop the gun," Brenna says. "Drop the gun, Darren, and we'll do as you say."

I'd expected this. Brenna is a master of making people believe what she wants them to.

"Good. No one else needs to get hurt," I say calmly. "Step away from the children, Brenna. You already killed Mark. I won't let you hurt them too."

I don't take my eyes off her, but I call out to Margot and Tobias, who are standing close together still, and watching all of this unfold. "The two of you need to take the children and get out of here. *Now*."

I press on the last word, trying to say it in a way that won't scare Felix and Daphne any more than they already are.

Brenna holds up her hands and moves away from everyone

else, towards the shelves and bathroom door. Felix stands and reaches his arm to his sister, who grabs it and lets him lift her.

"I don't understand," Margot says. "What the hell is happening?" She shifts her head from the children to Brenna to me, and back again. "Who's coming? Brenna, what's going on?"

I try to explain. "My friends are coming to burn down Granfield. We need to get out of here."

Tobias holds on to the kids and makes his way to the door with them. Brenna isn't moving, but her body is coiled, all pent-up energy waiting to burst. "What friends? Why are they burning Granfield down?" Tobias' voice sounds fragile, and he clears his throat a few times before he can get the words out.

"Do you want to tell them, or do you want me to?" I ask my partner in crime, who was never a partner. Brenna shrugs, a small movement that barely registers.

"There's nothing to tell." She hoists her chin up into the air. "I don't know why you're doing this, but please—don't hurt the children."

"I'd never hurt them," I remind her. "You know that."

Tobias and Margot are almost to the door, but they have to walk by Mark's body with the children and Tobias hesitates and scans the room, as though suddenly there will be a new path for him to take in this crowded violent space.

And that's when I do it. I look away for a second, tracing the outline of Mark's corpse with my gaze and trying to think of a way for the children to be safe and not have to see their father's dead body as they get there.

Brenna pulls out the handgun she must have taken from Mark. The one I should have figured she had as soon as I saw his limp body on the ground.

Now we're in a standoff, with our weapons raised at each other.

"You said that no one would get hurt," I remind her. "You

said that it was just a way to get more money from Mark's company, in order to save your own. The kidnapping ransom would be enough to pay off the guys, give me a nice bonus, and then fix all your problems. You knew—you knew how in debt I was after my little girl was sick, and you took advantage of it."

I feel the weight of the lives behind me, the children and the nurse and the horse whisperer. I can't let them get hurt any more than they already are.

"But then it came to the actual night, and I saw what you were really capable of. I saw you on the stairs that night, when Tobias got me from my apartment and told me we needed to rescue your family. I came, planning to fix it somehow that they got away, but then you were on the stairs and the look on your face was so satisfied, so greedy for what that thug was about to do that I knew there was never a plan to kidnap Mark. You were always going to kill him. So when Tobias fired in self-defense, I followed his lead."

I can't help it. I look at Mark's body. "And now Mark is dead, because of you."

She ignores my accusations. Margot and Tobias hold on to the children, both of them scanning the room between Brenna and me like they're spectators to some horrifying tennis match.

"So why'd you stay on for so many more months?" Brenna asks me. "Why didn't you turn me in if you knew my husband's life was in danger?"

"I was a fool, and a coward." I won't keep it inside any longer. There's no point in trying to hide who I am. "I convinced myself that maybe Mark was really sick, and that you were changed somehow and dedicated to caring for him. That was easier for me to believe, instead of having to face that I didn't go to the police or tell the truth because I wasn't willing to go to prison for what I'd done. I wanted to keep my pathetic small life here at Granfield."

SARAH K. STEPHENS

"And then you got sick, and it was the perfect way to get rid of you," Brenna goes on. "Right? That's what you want us all to think, isn't it? That I somehow made up this illness and this quarantine just so that I could get rid of you."

"No one thinks that," Margot says from across the room, a sudden hard edge to her voice. "We wouldn't have stayed here, locked away for weeks and almost starving, just because you told us to. We saw the news reports, we got the alerts on our phones. We couldn't contact our families because their towns were dealing with it even worse than we were, and the cellular service was disrupted. There's no way you could have faked all of this for us."

"But she did," I tell them all. "Brenna made it all up."

56

FELIX

Something breaks inside my head and I can't see for a minute, and then it all comes back in a rush of terrible, horrible things.

Dad lying there, his lips blue and looking up at me but not seeing me.

Tobias tries to shift his body in front of mine, blocking my view, and I feel more than see Margot doing the same thing for Daphne, but Tobias isn't tall enough if I stand on my tiptoes. I've grown over the last few weeks, and I can still see everything that's happening in this room where my father was supposed to be getting better and coming back to life.

Mom's hunched over in the corner like some creature from the movies I like to watch, trapped and waiting to bite. It was how the fox looked, when I caught it in the snare I set in the back field. I didn't want it bothering the horses anymore. Nipping at their legs in the dark.

It really bothered Daphne.

Darren's going to shoot her. He's going to shoot Mom.

I need to do something. But it's like Margot all over again. I'm frozen in place. Daphne squeezes my hand, and I can't even do that. I can't even squeeze back to lie to my sister so she thinks it's going to be okay.

Because it's not. Not ever again.

And even though there are things that can be done to help, I know there's nothing *I'll* be able to do to fix it. Because I'm like my father, jumping out the window to get away from his problems and leaving us all here, alone.

I'm a coward.

57

BRENNA

"I'll explain everything later. Just get them out of here!" Darren barks, and Margot and Tobias seem to wake from a daze. Margot slips a key card out of her pants pocket and the insistent click of the key reader unlocking and opening the door echoes through the room.

But I don't want them to leave. I don't want them to leave me alone with Darren. And, even more potent, churning underneath everything that's happened in this life of mine, I don't want my children to see me like this, defeated by some farmhand.

They need to know that I was powerful. That I was in control. It might be the last lesson I ever teach them. I can't let their final thoughts of me be that I was weak.

"Darren's right," I say. "I made up the quarantine." It must be a testament to how much they've already been through today, because nothing shifts across the faces of Tobias and Margot. Daphne and Felix stare at their shoes, like they can't hear me. So I keep going.

"There *is* a virus, and there was the order across the country to shelter-in-place, but there's still food in the grocery stores and hospitals are open. People can even get their food delivered, or order clothes online to wear in front of whoever they're sheltering with, like a new suit of armor against this microscopic invader. We were never going to starve, and we didn't have to be alone, out here waiting for it all to end."

Margot speaks first, like I knew she would.

"Why?" she murmurs, not making eye contact with me.

Tobias looks up and stares at me dead on. I stare right back. I'm not afraid of him.

"Because I needed Granfield Manor to feel isolated and disconnected from resources. It's the same thing you do when you need to acquire a competing company. You create discord in their own organization, so they start to eat away at each other from the inside, and then when everything is ready to crumble, you swoop in with an offer that's well below asking price and come out the winner. I needed all of you to turn on each other. To start suspecting the others of trying to hurt you. After I convinced you all that Darren was sick and contagious, and he was dead thanks to Tobias—he was *supposed* to be dead—it became that much easier to pit you and Tobias against one another."

"I took care of Margot," Tobias growls. "I carried her across that field and I dressed her wounds."

"Did you?" I ask him. "Because, on my count, Margot broke several ribs under your watch, and you were the one who discovered that bloody altar in the woods. Somebody killed a fox in your stable, sliced it through the neck with medical precision, you said, and then the greenhouse burned down without any witnesses. It wasn't that hard to spread fear. It's what human beings are built for—keying in on those tiny clues from other people that something is off. That you're in danger."

Felix doesn't move, but Daphne has lost interest in her shoes and her eyes meet mine in two whirling pools of blue. I've never seen her look so lost. My girl, the tough angel I molded.

"Plus, there was the added benefit that Tobias had a criminal background, like Darren." I scan Margot's face, and a riptide of shock moves over her features. She didn't know, which is good. "He tried to kill the man his wife was sleeping with. Not quite the same as Darren's drug kingpin helper, but it would be enough on paper to make anyone suspicious."

Darren holds the gun at me level and steady, but he doesn't seem to be so rushed anymore. In the past, before everything went to hell, he always seemed to like when I talked.

"Let's go," Margot says, gripping Daphne's hand and holding on to her own side as she steps through the open doorway. "You shouldn't hear this. This isn't right. We need to go!"

I can't believe I slept with her. And now she's touching my daughter.

"And Margot, you look exactly like your sister. I can't believe you thought you could come here and care for my husband and think that neither of us would recognize you. I knew who you were from the moment I hired you. Your last name is common enough—Miller—but your dark hair. Those cheekbones. Of course you were Teresa's sister. And you were so terribly overqualified to come and work here as a nurse to one patient. It was like you'd fallen into my lap, just when I needed you. So, when this is all over, even the kindly, compassionate nurse won't be above the police considering her a murderer too."

Margot's face goes pale. "What do you mean, I look like my sister?"

"I knew her—we were friends, in fact—when she was dating Mark. Of course, that didn't last for long, did it?"

Her mouth opens and closes, but no words come out.

I keep going, because I don't have time to wait for what I've said to register in Margot's mind fully.

I tell this last part to my children. To Daphne, in particular, because Felix won't look at me. "It was all going to plan. You see, I built something in this world." I crouch down, so I'm level with my daughter. I steal a glance up at Felix, and he swings his eyes towards me for a few moments before blinking them away again. "My company has changed the lives of so many people. It helps keep families together, you see? It brings people closer. It changed the world, and it showed other women—girls like you, sweetheart—that they could be leaders too. But it was in trouble, because of some bad people." I leave out the part where I made some poor investments and avoided some user privacy protocols, and the millions of dollars in fines we'd accrued because of it.

"I needed to save it, for the other women out there who were counting on me lifting them up. I couldn't let them get hurt because I failed. Do you understand?"

Darren takes a deep breath, and his nostrils flare as he exhales. He's letting me finish. He's going to let me finish.

"So I was willing to sacrifice everything to help the people who needed me. And I knew you would, too. You'd want to help."

"I love helping you, Mommy," Daphne's voice sounds so small compared to mine. "I always do what you tell me."

"Is that why you poisoned her?" The words scratch out of Felix's mouth like sandpaper. He seems surprised that he even spoke.

So my boy figured it out. Of course he did.

"I needed you both to help me, so that I could save the company," I say it meekly, and I feel the weight of it as the words come out. But I don't regret it. They have a right to know that, even though I loved them, I couldn't protect them from the way the world works.

Tobias hasn't moved an inch since I started. He's listening

too, like Darren. I've always had a power over men. "So you were going to kill your husband and your children, and place the blame on us? Why?"

"I needed a clean slate. I need all of Mark's money in order to save my company. I can't split it with the children—it would stay in trust for at least fifteen years for both of them."

"You did it for money." Darren emphasizes the last word.

"I did it for the future," I snap back.

"When everything was finished, all of you with your crimes and dangerous backgrounds would be blamed for what happened here at Granfield. I'd be the victim of your horrible plan—whether it was Margot taking down all Mark's family and friends in order to get revenge, or Tobias not being able to handle the pressures of life outside prison and contain his violent rages. Or, maybe Darren's buddies came for revenge, as payback for abandoning them. There were so many different options, thanks to your messy lives. Any of those would have worked, depending on how it all played out. But in the end, I'd be left alone, and I'd be able to save myself."

I say it, but I don't feel the words anymore. Daphne has started to cry. Felix stares at a corner of the ceiling.

You can always have more children, I remind myself. They deserved to know.

"That's enough," Darren decides. He moves to the door, shotgun still leveled at me, and as I watch from the side I see my children, my lover, and my only friends leave me locked here, with my dead husband by my side.

58

DARREN

"Get to the panic room!" I shout. I have to risk leaving Brenna there, locked in. I need to make sure they get to the room safely.

Because the string of windows along the hallway tells me it's already happening.

Four long shiny black SUVs are parked in the gravel lot behind the house. There's the sound of scraping outside along the walls.

They're here, and they're setting it all up. Kindle and flame. Gasoline soaking into the foundation of the house. They'll be thorough. After last time, they're not letting anything go to chance.

If we go outside, they'll shoot us. No witnesses. They kept telling me that, when we'd meet on Brenna's laptop. I risked getting caught, time and time again, to use the terrible things I've done to do one thing right, until she finally did catch me.

The panic room is fireproof, with its own special supply of air, like it was always inevitable that Granfield would burn.

Felix whimpers as we race to the solid metal doors seated inside the center of the house. He's been so quiet for most of this, but now a dam seems to be breaking and everything inside of him pours out.

I used to do that when I was a kid. I still do it now, alone in my apartment before all of this, thinking of my little girl and the cancer that ate away at her body until she wasn't much more than a shell of the happy, round and bouncing baby that she once was. When she died, she was three, but looked like she was maybe twelve, eighteen months and like she'd been through a famine and a civil war. Which she had, in a way. Her body fighting itself. I couldn't do anything besides sit in that molded plastic chair and hold her to me. There was no magic, no strings that my rich criminal friends could pull, no people to know that could save her.

But today, I can correct that past a little. I can save Felix and Daphne. I can make sure their mother never hurts them again. After the fire, no one will come looking for them to settle scores or take their money. They'll be safe. They can live good normal lives after this.

We're almost there. The clangs and crashes from what the men are doing outside won't reach them once they're inside the room. It'll be peaceful in there.

A loud crunch of metal against metal splits the air, and we all flinch at the sudden burst of sound. I don't dare to glance out of the window, because I know what the rising noise means. Granfield is made of stone, and so they knew to use the machines from the farm shed, and where the keys were, to drive them to the house and knock holes in the foundations. They'll set the flames in those pockets, and then watch the building, and everyone in it, burn.

We get to the room, Tobias leading us and Margot and I taking up the end, Margot leaning on me but moving as fast as she can, with the two children in the middle. Felix is crying full force and Daphne is stoic, sucking on her thumb like she used to do when she was younger. I punch in the code to unlatch the door, and like in the medical wing, the locks give a soft hiss as everything unfurls and the cool, padded sanctuary of the panic room opens itself to us.

It has to be this way. They're here for revenge, like I am. No witnesses. No survivors.

We all have to die. It's just that some of us are going to be reborn.

Margot settles Daphne on one of the seats and Felix stumbles into the spot next to her. Tobias stands in the doorway, not inside the room yet.

"What are all those sounds?" he asks me. I try to move through the doorway, to get one last look at Felix and Daphne, but he blocks me with his shoulders and puts a hand out to push against my chest.

"What happens when we close ourselves in here?" he goes on.

"I have to finish things," I tell him. "None of you need to be a part of this. I started it. I'm going to end it."

"You can't go back by yourself." Tobias moves through the doors. "I need to help you."

Margot stands and comes up behind him. "The children will be safe here. We can both help you. We can still stop this— whatever this is." She pauses, and then says more quietly, "We can still stop her."

There's a steely flint to Margot's expression that passes across her face, and it's like she wants me to know that she's not talking about stopping Brenna from leaving the house or from going to the police. She's talking about stopping her, forever.

Margot's gaze shifts to wrap around the room, but there aren't any windows to see the men working on burning us to the ground. She'll have seen the cars and the gasoline as we ran through the halls. Both of them must know what's about to happen, what I need to do.

"What do you need us to do?" Margot echoes my thoughts back to me.

I have to move quickly. I have to make sure they understand me but that they don't follow me.

"I need you to stay here until it's over, and then I need you to take the children far away from here. No one can know who they are."

I look at Margot, then at Tobias. They seem uncertain at first by what I'm saying, both of them leaning out and Margot reaching as if to grab onto something hovering between us. She drops her hands an instant later, as what I'm saying registers. Tobias shakes his head, but I continue.

"Keep them safe. Start a new life. Leave Granfield behind them. Help them forget it ever existed. Don't leave this room until they're gone and this is all over. Give the children a new life." I take a quick step back, drink in the image of Daphne and Felix behind them, and then push as hard as I can against Tobias. He falls backwards, unsteady on his feet.

"Keep them safe!" is the last thing I say to them as I swing the door closed, wait the moment for the locks to engage, and then punch in the twenty-digit override code to fasten the doors for twenty-four hours. Brenna insisted on having that installed, so the panic room could act as a prison cell if they ever needed it. "Granfield is so far away from town," she'd argued. "It'd take a long time for help to come."

I checked the air supply yesterday, before my final call on the laptop. They'll be safe until tomorrow, when everyone is gone. They'll be able to open the door, and walk out onto the foundation of the house and into new lives. Tobias will know how to get fake IDs and papers. Prison teaches you a lot of things.

We weren't cellmates, but we knew each other from the grounds outside when the guards gave us outdoor time. Same block. It's probably why he never liked me, because I knew he was a criminal, same as me.

I turn and take the hallway back to the stairs, across the house, and over to the west wing where Brenna's locked in with Mark's body. She might have tried to get out the window already, but I would have heard gunshots when the men outside opened fire to shoot her down.

"No witnesses," that steely voice kept saying through the screen, accented in strange places that sounded like my mother but were entirely different at the same time. His voice was all weight and metal compared to my mother's lightness.

I can smell the smoke now, burning through the holes in the stone they've made. There's a rumbling in the bottom of the house, as though a giant is waking.

It's the flames, coming like a train down a track, eating everything they can touch.

I'm ready, I think as I reach the door and open it with my key card. The fire will melt down the system. The police won't be able to tell that I was the last one in here, or who was coming and going these last days and weeks. They'll just know that the fire was hungry and took everything, and everyone, with it.

59

TOBIAS

I pound on the door, press all the release buttons, but nothing will budge.

The room feels like it's closing around me. I can't breathe.

"Put your head between your legs," Margot advises, her hand pressed flat against my back. She lays it gently, and I feel the pain from her broken ribs course through her to me as she tries to calm me down, even as she's dealing with being locked away by someone we thought was dead too.

The first scents of smoke start to filter through the vents.

What's Darren planning to do?

I take breaths as deeply as I can manage, shallow and raking at first and then deeper as the seconds pass.

What about the horses? I think. *What will they do to my horses?*

"Isn't there a separate air supply in here?" Felix asks.

"I can't get us out." I fight the urge to slam my hands against the keyboard.

"Why can I smell smoke, if there are separate air supplies for this room?" Felix's voice breaks through the tangle of my thoughts. He gets up from his seat and moves to the video monitor. He taps at some buttons, and the view of the empty space outside the panic room's door appears. He taps some more, putting in different codes that seem longer than the ones Mark had me memorize, and different views appear, shifting from outside the door of the panic room to further inside the house, room to room. The rooms are empty, until Felix shifts to a camera outside the front door.

Black SUVs take up the screen, their bodies glinting like polished coffins in the sunlight. There are men with masks, running around with guns and gasoline tanks. The ones in the image we can see are loading back into the cars, but not driving away. Just waiting silently behind their tinted windows. A few stand outside, guns slung across their chests.

Smoke billows from the side of the screen.

They're burning us down.

"They're burning Granfield down," Margot echoes my thoughts. She turns to look at Daphne. "But we'll be safe here."

"Why is there smoke? Something's wrong!" Felix screams.

"I need to tell you something," a voice booms from the speakers in the top corners of the panic room. "Children, I need you to know one more thing."

"Mommy?" Daphne says.

They hear scraping across the speakers, and then Darren's voice comes through, but he's not speaking to them.

"It's time, Brenna," he says, quieter than Brenna's voice was over the speaker.

The intercom. The intercom through the house is on.

Felix presses a button on the display. "Mom! Darren! You need to come help us! The air supply isn't working. We're going to suffocate. Please come and help us!"

"Stop it," Daphne cries.

"But I checked," Darren says, almost to himself it seems. His voice is weaker still than before.

"Help us!" Felix cries again.

There are more sounds in the intercom, something brushing up against the microphone, and then a loud crack, like a firework being let off against the speaker.

60

BRENNA

I t was almost too easy.

Distracting Darren as he arrived back in the room. I would have tried to sneak out the window, but I knew he was coming back and I couldn't leave him as a loose end, any more than I could have Tobias, Margot, and the children.

My children.

Now he's dead on the floor, shot through the back of his head when he turned round to go back and save everyone, like a hero. I tuck my gun into the waistband of my pants, but I leave the bulky shotgun on the ground near Darren's body.

Now I need to escape.

The house is on fire. Darren's guys, who were my guys, must have set it up.

The panic room's air supply is turned off. I took care of that late last night. I had a sense that Darren was back—I thought I caught a glimpse of him, in the trees, when I set the greenhouse on fire and before I went back to the house to pretend like I didn't know it was burning. And before that, Margot said she saw a man in the woods. If he was here, if Tobias hadn't killed him and he hadn't died from the virus, I wasn't about to let him create a room that was perfectly safe from anything and anyone.

That wouldn't work. Not at all.

I take one more look at Mark's body, the smoke coming in like curtains from the floor and ceiling. Something jerks inside of me and I almost lean down to kiss his lips, one last time, but I don't. They would be hard and cold set by now.

He's not in there, anyway. It's just a body.

I quickly unfurl the sheet from around his neck and fling it out the window. It's held securely to the bedpost where I tied it earlier.

No one will survive this.

Except for me.

I have money—so much money. They won't shoot me, because I can pay them more than they ever dreamed of.

Nothing is more important to a person than money.

I climb out the window, hoisting myself against the stone and propelling my body down. The flames haven't burned through this portion of the house yet. When I reach the ground, I stand up straight, smooth my hair, and walk over to the man positioned at the lead car with the biggest gun.

"I'm Brenna Stone," I tell him.

My name seems to register. Even though his mask obscures his face, something changes in the set of his shoulders.

"I'll pay you double whatever Darren promised you if you let me walk away, right now. I can make you richer than your wildest dreams."

There's no time to run. No time to negotiate and talk my way out of this. No time to grab my gun and defend myself. The man, the leader, lifts his weapon and shoots me in the chest. I fall back, blood rising up my throat and leeching out of my body. All the power I've collected over my entire life, all the choices I've made to get me here and make me stronger, drip into the pristine white gravel below.

I want to hurl out a scream for the total waste of it, but blood catches in my throat.

The man who shot me takes off his mask. I don't recognize him at first, although there's something in the cut of his face that seems familiar, like an echo of a memory from long ago.

He leans down, and whispers into my ear.

"My brother died, trying to kidnap your husband," he tells me. "Some things are worth more than being rich. And now, I'm going to watch you die, like you deserve."

I have nothing to say. I couldn't even if I wanted to persuade him otherwise. Blood fills my mouth.

One thought ricochets around my head: I don't deserve this.

61

FELIX

We're going to die in this stupid claustrophobic room.

Smoke pours in and the metal joints at the top of the walls are getting hotter and turning from grey steel to a strange amber color from the heated air the fire is making. Even though the walls are fireproof, the ventilation needs to be switched over to the separate system in order to keep the smoke from getting in and igniting.

People don't realize that there are particles in the smoke that catch fire.

I think Darren's dead. Or maybe it's Mom. I don't know. Margot and Tobias keep jabbering away, offering suggestions of what to type into the keypad to get us out of here or to get the air working. I can't listen to them though, and their words melt together like they're being heated by the fire.

We're all coughing, and Margot shouts out instructions that seem to be about covering up our faces with our shirts and crouching down lower in the room. The floor feels cool to the touch, and I press my head against it and wait for all of this to be over.

Daphne just stares into space. She hasn't said a word since

Mom called out from the speakers and we heard that crack of the bullet or whatever it was.

I can't fool myself. I know it was a gunshot. I'm sure Daphne does too.

The metal grate presses its indents into my cheek and I push harder and harder until it scrapes the inside of my mouth against my teeth. Margot keeps saying things in her calm nurse voice and Tobias has wrapped a blanket around the four of us.

"It's going to be okay," Margot whispers. "We're going to be okay."

Tobias pulls Daphne and me under his chest, like somehow he's going to shield us from the smoke and the heat that's about to kill us.

I thought Darren was helping us, but I think he locked us in here to hurt us. Maybe he switched off the air? And then he locked us in.

Or maybe he thought we'd be the safest here, and there's been an accident. The air just won't work. Or somebody turned it off.

Mom's face, back in Dad's room with his body lying on the floor—I didn't want to look, I wasn't going to look, but then I did and I can't picture Dad at all except for that bluish face and his twisted mouth staring back at me from the floor—telling us all how she was willing to sacrifice Daphne and me and everyone else at Granfield so her stupid company could survive.

Daphne reaches out and squeezes my hand. This time I squeeze back. Her words cut through the pounding drums inside my head.

"People don't see me," she whispers in my ear. "They don't notice that I'm there."

Before Tobias can stop her, Daphne squirms out from under his hold and from the blanket. I have a deep scream that rises inside my body and pours out as she disappears outside the blanket's edges.

"No!" I cry out to her. I can't lose her too.

But a second later, while I try to fight against Tobias to let me go, there's a change in the room that shifts the entire smoking world around us.

High-pitched beeps and then a loud shudder, followed by whirring fans kicking on.

Daphne reappears under the blanket, her face flushed but shining. She's actually smiling.

"I fixed it," she tells us.

"Come here, let me look at you." Margot reaches out to her.

"You don't need to be under there anymore. We're going to be okay," Daphne explains.

A deep stab of something worse than dying forms in the pit of my stomach.

I pull myself out from under the blanket, and sure enough the air is clear and the walls are turning back to their cool steel selves.

"I remembered the override code to switch the air on. I saw Mom do it." Daphne shrugs, like us almost burning alive and everything else that's happened to us these last two days have been no big deal, now that she's fixed everything.

"She didn't think I'd remember." Daphne sits down in the same place where she sat the night our mother had us stay in here when Darren was sick.

She turns her face to me, where I'm still crouched on the floor of the room, and pats the seat next to her.

Margot and Tobias do a quick assessment of the room and the controls, careful not to really touch anything, and then they sit down across from Daphne.

I stay on the floor, waiting. I'm certain—more certain than I've ever been of anything—of what's coming next.

"You saved us, Daphne." Margot looks around at all of us, crowded together and surviving. "You did it."

I climb up, but I don't sit next to my sister.

I saved her—I saved Margot first, from the terrible thing Daphne did to her. But no one will remember that now.

All they'll remember is Daphne, rescuing us.

So I just stare out through the video monitor, waiting for it to be over.

62

MARGOT

The next several hours pass by in a blur. We wait and we talk sometimes, at least Tobias and Daphne and I do—Felix stands in a corner, staring at the screens—and then sometimes we sit quietly.

There are sounds that make it into the room. Crashes and rumbles as Granfield Manor burns around us, but we are secure and safe.

The hours tick by and I sense a shift in Tobias. He's getting ready for the next part.

We don't talk about it, but I know we're in agreement with what will happen after we leave this place. Daphne and Felix are our responsibilities now. So we need to do what's right, and what's right is to not leave the children to fend for themselves.

What's right is to not let Darren risk everything for us, after we risked nothing for him.

I don't know what part Brenna played in Teresa's death, but I'm certain she *was* part of it in some way, and that Mark isn't to blame.

My body aches and my throat burns, from everything that's happened to me here at Granfield Manor and from everything that brought me here in the first place. The guilt for coming to Granfield to hurt Mark is a heavy chain around my neck. Maybe I'll grow stronger as I get used to it, and it'll become like another part of my body. But I already know it won't ever go away.

Like the shame I have for sleeping with Brenna, for not protecting Darren when he was ill, for not recognizing the signs that Brenna was poisoning Mark's body like she was poisoning her children's minds. Life can't just be a sum of a person's mistakes, can it? Of the harms we've caused others?

Maybe Tobias is thinking the same thing. That this is a new beginning for both of us. We can redeem ourselves.

I don't know if what Brenna said about Tobias is true. She was right about me. Maybe she was telling the truth about Tobias too. But something tells me Tobias won't hurt me. He tried to protect Daphne from the virus, and he couldn't bring himself to hurt Darren. He carried me across those fields so carefully.

Then again, I haven't been the best judge of character lately.

And of course, he could be wondering the same thing about me. He'd have every right to, after what I've done.

We'll have to trust each other if we're going to get through this.

I can't let any of that get in the way—not suspicions, not anger, and especially not grief. There's no room for any of that now, because there are two children who need me. Need *us*— Tobias and me. I have to be strong and loving and good for them.

Children can recover from almost anything. I think I'm living proof of that, and hopefully Daphne and Felix will be too, one day.

There's no time to look back. There's only moving forward.

EPILOGUE

SIX MONTHS LATER

Felix

I told the teacher I needed to use the bathroom. She let me go because she knows I'm not one of those kids who goes to the bathroom to goof around with their friends.

My new school isn't as fancy as the one I went to when I was still Felix. After the fire, Margot and Tobias took us in Margot's car—Tobias knew how to start it without the key—and drove for hours and hours. We didn't see my mother, but I knew she was dead. I felt it, inside my chest like a fist clenching around the muscle of my heart and then releasing.

Tobias kept calling people and hanging up, and then calling them back until I heard him talk to someone about payments and papers. I thought maybe Tobias was checking about the horses, who were all safe in their stables—he made us look before we left—and waiting for someone to come get them. And maybe he did call somebody about the horses, some anonymous call to make sure they were taken care of, but most of those calls

I think were about new names and identification and getting access to money he'd been saving for a long time somewhere secret. I remember he talked about insurance money from a woman named Colleen, who I think might have been his wife.

Margot drove and drove until we ended up in this little town where we rented a house, and then a few days later Daphne and I started school and we were supposed to call Margot "Mom" and Tobias "Dad" in front of other people, to go along with the story they were telling our teachers and our neighbors.

I don't mind it so much. Margot and Tobias are really nice to Daphne and me, and they seem to like each other, although they don't kiss or sleep in the same room. Sometimes I'll come out after dinner, when all the lights are turned low in our little house, and see them sitting at the kitchen table, talking and smiling at each other.

Margot and Tobias told us we shouldn't look it up, but I did anyway one day, when I was at the library after school—that way my searches wouldn't be traceable, if someone did come looking for us in this tiny town with one stoplight and a postage-stamp-sized library. I searched for Granfield Manor, and then I searched for Brenna Stone. The first articles said that Granfield Manor had burned down and that it was believed to be arson. Everyone in the house was suspected to have died, although they only found the remains for three people. Everyone else supposedly burned up.

Before we left, Tobias set fire to the inside of the panic room. It burned extra hot, because it was so well insulated.

The papers had pictures of Tobias from a horse show he'd done with Jasmine, her mane all shiny and combed out, a few years ago. Margot's nursing graduation photo was next to mine and Daphne's school pictures from that year. Dad's picture was the one from his company's website. The fire made some of the bigger papers. The police suspected the Russian mob, because, the reports said, of ties to one of the workers at Granfield, Darren Stuyven.

When I searched my mother's name, I only found a few articles about how her company was being taken over by her second-in-command, someone named Ivan Ratchkov. Dad's company went into trust with his executive board. There was one line, at the end of an article, that mentioned the money. "If the Stones children had lived, they would stand to inherit almost $10 million in stock investments and other financial assets, not to mention the insurance money for Granfield Manor itself."

I wash my hands in the sink and stare up at my face. We have to wear masks at school to cover our mouth and nose. I wear normal ones that Margot got for us at the grocery store. They're all blue and make it hot to breathe in, but other kids wear the same ones too, so I don't stand out for being weird or poor.

And we're not poor. We're just not rich either.

We're normal, at least on the outside. I'm normal. I like being that, for now. I have a few friends in my class, and sometimes I go over to their houses to play video games or eat dinner. I have to wear my mask there too.

You get used to it.

It's strange though, wearing the mask, because it makes you notice people's faces in a different way from when you can see all of them. Daphne looks almost exactly like Mom, with the same blue eyes and soft pretty forehead.

When I look at myself in the mirror, at first I thought I looked like Dad, but then I remembered that Mom was the one who always told me I looked like him. And Mom was a liar. So I kept looking at my face, and I realized that I didn't look anything like my father.

I've been practicing remembering him like he was, before he

got sick and before he died in that room. Before my mother killed him, that is.

My eyes are dark and wide-set. My hair falls in a strange way across my forehead, and it's darker than anyone else's in my family. I was at home, staring into the mirror with my mask on, trying to figure out what kept bothering me when I'd see my reflection. And then I knew, all of sudden. Like when I finally understood that gravity accelerates rather than staying constant.

I remembered those eyes, looking at me and telling me that I needed to be safe. Making Margot and Tobias promise to give me a new life.

That's when I knew that Daphne was the good child, and always would be. She saved us because she's only half bad. She's half Mom, sure, but she's also half Dad. And Dad was a good person.

But me. I'm all bad. My mother only cared about herself, and my real father, Darren, was willing to burn my home—our home—down to the ground in order to get back at my mother. He was willing to lock us in a room with no air so he could be the hero himself.

I dry my hands on the disposable towels and push the door open with my foot, like my teacher taught me.

When I step out into the hallway, it's deserted. I could go back to my classroom, and back to my lessons.

But what if I made a quick stop somewhere else—maybe the janitor's closet or the teacher's bathroom or my sister's locker? What if I decided to stop fighting who I really am?

Because I'm not the hero of this story.

I'll always be something else.

THE END

ACKNOWLEDGEMENTS

Thank you to Bloodhound Books for seeing this project through to its final version. This novel began as a work of writing therapy for me during the early days of the Covid-19 pandemic. It grew into the novel it is today through the support of Bloodhound's fantastic team.

Thank you to my writing friends, including J.L. Delozier and Brian Centrone.

Jen, thanks for always being the Thelma to my Louise (or am I Thelma?).

Brian, thank you for texting luxury fashion sale items to my phone. You're right—fashion and friendship are life-affirming.

Thank you to my dear friend, Jennifer Crissman-Ishler, for being my best work buddy and all around go-to friend when anything is happening in life, good or bad.

Thank you to one of my first English teachers, Mrs. Lipiatt, for encouraging my writing from such an early age.

Thank you to my Mom for loving me, encouraging me, chatting with me on my walks, showing me great hiking trails, and just being an awesome mom and grandma.

Thank you to my late father, Stephen. I live my life each day trying to follow your example.

Thank you to my children for letting me be a part of their lives as they grow into young adults and get ready to explore the world.

Finally, thank you to my husband, Joshua, for all your years of love.

ABOUT THE AUTHOR

Sarah K. Stephens is the author of four novels and a developmental psychologist at Penn State University. Her writing has appeared in *LitHub*, *The Writer's Chronicle*, *Hazlitt*, and *The Millions*. Aside from *Isolation*, her books include the psychological thrillers *A Flash of Red*, *It Was Always You*, and *The Anniversary*. Sarah lives with her husband and children in Central Pennsylvania.

Follow Sarah on Twitter (@skstephenswrite), Instagram (@skstephenswrite), or Facebook (@sarahkstephensauthor) and read more of her writing on her website (www.sarahkstephens.com).